Samantha's life would never be the same again. . . .

"I'm going out to the barn to tie up some loose ends," Samantha's father said.

Samantha jumped up. It was the day after her mother's funeral and she'd been sitting in her room for hours, rearranging the makeup and brushes on her bureau. "I want to go with you." *Mom would want me to go out to the horses.*

Ian sighed. "Okay, come on." He smiled a little. "I can use the company."

Samantha hurried out to the truck before he could change his mind.

"Look, Sammy . . ." Ian cleared his throat. "When we get to the barn, I want you to be very careful when I'm not with you."

"I'm always careful—you know that, Dad." Why was her father making such an obvious point?

Ian sighed deeply. "That's not exactly what I mean, Sammy. I don't want you around the horses without supervision. And . . . I don't want you to ride anymore."

Collect all the books in the Thoroughbred series

Collect all the books in the Ashleigh series

* coming soon

THOROUGHBRED

SAMANTHA'S JOURNEY

CREATED BY
JOANNA CAMPBELL

WRITTEN BY
KAREN BENTLEY

HarperPaperbacks
A Division of HarperCollins*Publishers*

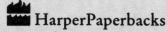 HarperPaperbacks
A Division of HarperCollins*Publishers*
10 East 53rd Street, New York, N.Y. 10022-5299

This is a work of fiction. The characters, incidents, and
dialogues are products of the author's imagination and are not to
be construed as real. Any resemblance to actual events or
persons, living or dead, is entirely coincidental.

❖ 10 9 8 7 6 5

—to John—

SAMANTHA'S JOURNEY

Prologue

SAMANTHA MCLEAN WALKED BRISKLY ALONG HER FAVORITE riding trail at Whitebrook, the exclusive Thoroughbred breeding and training farm where she lived. She glanced up at the bright blue sky and smiled broadly. "I can't believe it," she said aloud. "I'm really going to be a trainer at Whitebrook!"

She paused next to a large oak tree and hugged herself with sheer delight. The tree branches, bursting with April leaves, formed a soft, swaying green arch over her head. The woods were silent except for the cheerful chatter of birds, and the cool air carried the sweet scent of violets and rhododendron. The familiar forest seemed as happy and bright as her future.

Samantha replayed the scene that had just taken place in Mike Reese's office. Her dad, Ian McLean, and Mike, Whitebrook's owner, had formally offered her a job as assistant trainer at the farm. It was what Sam had been hoping for almost her whole life.

"I'll train so many different kinds of horses," Samantha murmured. "There are always great young horses coming to Whitebrook. But maybe when I have enough experience, I can take a chance and buy a horse at auction, like Shining."

Samantha closed her eyes, enjoying the warm sunshine on her face. "Finding the next Kentucky Derby winner in an overlooked colt will be my specialty!" she vowed.

"May I join this conversation?" asked a familiar, deep voice.

Samantha opened her eyes to see Tor Nelson, her longtime boyfriend, walking toward her. She couldn't help but smile as she watched him approach. With his tall, athletic build, blond hair, and intense blue eyes, Samantha thought he was the handsomest guy she'd ever seen. More important, he shared her love of horses. Together they'd trained Whitebrook's famous steeplechaser, Sierra.

"Where have you been?" Samantha asked. "I have great news."

Tor sat down, pulling her to the ground with him. "I was talking to Shining."

"Oh, really? What were you two discussing?" Samantha raised an eyebrow. Samantha talked to the horses all the time, especially Shining, but Tor wasn't usually so fanciful.

"It can wait," Tor said. "Tell me your news."

Samantha thought Tor almost sounded relieved. Now she was really curious about what he had been saying to Shining. "No," she said, shaking her head. "You go first."

Tor cleared his throat.

Samantha stared at Tor, her excitement over her new job replaced by a tightening in her stomach as she tried to read his expression. He looked happy and scared and determined all at once.

Tor looked intently into her eyes. "Samantha McLean, will you marry me?"

For a moment Samantha was so surprised, she couldn't speak. Her mouth dropped open, but nothing came out. She could feel her heart racing. *I guess I always dreamed that Tor and I would get married someday. But this is no dream—it's real.* Samantha shivered, despite the warm day.

"Hey," Tor said gently. "Say something; you're scaring me."

Samantha took a deep breath. *Say yes, you idiot. Just open your mouth and say yes. Everything about it will be good. You'll be here—at Whitebrook, with Tor—forever. You'll never be alone. . . .*

"You know I love you," Tor added, tenderly taking her hands in his.

Samantha felt a thrill of excitement race up her spine at Tor's words. What was she waiting for? Tor would be the most wonderful husband ever. She squeezed Tor's hands. "Yes!" she shouted joyfully. "I'll marry you!"

Tor jumped up and pulled Samantha to him for a quick, breathless kiss. "Let's go tell the others," he said eagerly.

"Okay!" Samantha grinned, imagining the surprised faces and congratulations from their friends and family. Grabbing Tor's hand, she ran with him out of the woods.

From her vantage point on the hill at the edge of the woods, Samantha had a clear view of all of Whitebrook. To her right was the mile-long exercise track. She could see her sister, Cindy, out on the track with the other riders. Her father; Ashleigh Griffin, Mike's wife and co-owner of Whitebrook; and Mike were standing along the rail watching the horses.

Samantha scanned the rest of the farm. The paddock closest to the barns was full of romping, running young foals, who had all been born this spring. My Hero, a gray colt and one of March to Glory's second crop of foals, was deliciously scratching his back on the ground, waving his long, slender legs in the air.

The young horse sprang to his feet, shook himself vigorously, and charged across the paddock, bucking and snorting at his playmates. *I know just how he feels.* Samantha grinned. *I'm so full of happiness, I could burst!*

Still grasping Tor's hand, Samantha started down

the hill toward the track. "Hey, Cindy!" Samantha called out as she approached.

Cindy nodded to show she'd heard the greeting, but she didn't take her attention off Honor Bright, the spirited filly she was exercising. The daughter of Ashleigh's Wonder, a Kentucky Derby and Breeders' Cup winner, Honor was the star two-year-old at Whitebrook. And, even at the best of times, she was a handful for her rider.

Ashleigh left her spot at the rail and walked over to Samantha. She squeezed her shoulder. "Mike told me you're officially coming on board at Whitebrook," she said, her hazel eyes warm. "I couldn't be happier, Sammy."

"Thanks!" Samantha hugged Ashleigh tight. Ashleigh, still only in her twenties, was one of the best Thoroughbred trainers and jockeys in the business. Her opinion meant the world to Samantha.

"Was that the news you were going to tell me?" Tor asked as Ashleigh rejoined Mike and Ian at the rail.

"Yes, but it's not as exciting as *our* news," Samantha replied. "Let's wait until Cindy is finished with Honor, then we can tell everyone."

She walked over and leaned on the track rail as she watched her sister ride. *Honor is definitely in one of her bad moods*, Samantha thought. The bay filly was yanking on the reins, trying to get her head, and skittering sideways across the track. Patiently Cindy straightened Honor out and urged her forward. Protesting the entire time, the filly broke into a reluctant gallop around the first turn.

Mike moved to the other side of Samantha and rested his foot on the bottom rail. "Honor's a handful today," he remarked.

Samantha nodded. "Honor's a real boss filly—and she's excitable. But I think Cindy can handle her."

Tor rested his chin on top of Samantha's head. "Listen to your new trainer. Cindy may be young, but she's learned fast and she definitely has a way with Honor."

"She *has* ridden Honor a couple of months now," Ian said, nodding. Samantha thought her father sounded concerned. She watched him closely as he picked up his binoculars to study horse and rider as they moved to the far side of the track.

Shrugging off an uneasy feeling that was forming in the pit of her stomach, Samantha turned her attention back to the track. Honor's glossy, thick black mane and tail floated luxuriously behind her. The filly's head jerked up as she rounded the far turn into the stretch, and her galloping strides lengthened.

"Slow her down, Cindy," Samantha murmured. Honor was moving in a straight line, but her strides were choppy and uneven.

A gust of wind blasted along the track. With a sharp snort, Honor dropped off the pace.

"Good, she's letting up a little," Mike said.

"No, she isn't!" Samantha stared at the track with growing apprehension. Honor was only getting ready to charge!

The filly seized the bit in her teeth and roared down the stretch at a full racing gallop. "No, Honor!" Cindy cried.

Samantha held her breath as Cindy hauled on the reins, struggling to slow the filly down. But Honor wasn't listening. Still moving at top speed, she veered across the track until she was headed straight at the inside rail!

"Cindy!" Samantha screamed, already over the fence and running across the soft, harrowed dirt of the track.

In the next second Honor's chest hit the rail and shattered it. Samantha saw what happened next very clearly, as if it were all happening in slow motion. Cindy was still desperately hanging on, but Honor was losing her balance, going to her knees as the pieces of broken rail dropped to the ground. The filly hit the inner turf course with a terrible thud, throwing Cindy over her head. Cindy rolled onto her back and lay still.

"Oh, my God," Ashleigh cried.

Samantha was almost to the infield. She threw herself to her knees at Cindy's side. Cindy hadn't moved, and her face was chalk white. "Cindy?" Samantha asked, her voice shaking. "Cindy!" She reached out to touch her sister.

"Don't move her," Ashleigh snapped, coming up beside Samantha. She knelt down next to Cindy and felt at her throat for a pulse.

Cindy's chest rose and fell in shallow breaths. Samantha was faintly aware of a horse's agonized groan and Tor's soothing murmurs as Honor struggled to rise.

"Mike, call 911!" Ashleigh put her ear next to Cindy's mouth. "She's stopped breathing. Tor, help me do CPR."

Samantha turned and buried her face in her father's shoulder. Ian was as pale as Cindy. He gently held her lifeless hand in his. "You'll be fine, baby. You'll be just fine," he repeated softly.

Samantha inhaled with a sharp, terrified sob. A flood of images flashed through Samantha's mind. She remembered a perfect spring day and a beautiful bay horse running wild across the track at a training farm in Florida. She remembered her father saying the same words over and over. . . .

Cindy is dead, Samantha thought wildly. *Just like Mom. She's dead!* Samantha staggered to her feet and shook her head hard, but she couldn't stop the surge of memories. Her mother lying on the ground, pale and still; her father kneeling beside her, holding her hand . . .

An ambulance rolled across the grass in eerie silence. Two heavyset male ambulance attendants rolled a stretcher up to Cindy and quickly loaded her on it. In shock, Samantha watched as Ian climbed in behind his daughter.

"I'll never see Cindy alive again," Samantha whispered. Her mind was reeling. She knew she'd go crazy if she had to watch this scene for another minute—she was already going crazy.

Samantha ran blindly toward the barns, tripping over uneven patches of ground. Over the roaring in her ears she thought she heard Tor's voice, but she couldn't wait for him.

"I have to get away," Samantha panted as she careened around the corner into the mares' barn.

Just a few feet away Shining popped her roan head over her stall half door. The mare looked hopeful and a little impatient. Ordinarily she would have been out in the paddock long before now. She didn't understand that this wasn't an ordinary day at all.

Overwhelmed, Samantha ran to Shining's stall. She let herself in, closed the stall door, and huddled in a corner, weeping hopelessly into her hands. Shining whoofed gently in her hair, as if she sensed Samantha's distress.

"Oh, Shining." Samantha put her trembling hand on the mare's black muzzle. "I can't bear it if Cindy's gone, too. I'm not strong enough to find happiness again." She hugged her knees, resting her back against the stall wall.

Shining gently nudged her shoulder, as if to encourage her to go on.

"How can I marry Tor?" Samantha moaned. "I was a fool to think I could be that happy. And now Cindy's dead, and my life will be so sad.... Oh, Shining, I'm afraid. The way Cindy fell . . . I can't stop remembering. . . ."

"WHAT A PERFECT DAY!" TWELVE-YEAR-OLD SAMANTHA exclaimed as she urged Miracle Worker into a trot on the track at Ivor Stables, a training farm near Miami.

"That it is," her mom agreed, trotting the horse she was riding, Gulfstream Waves, up alongside Miracle Worker. The warm Florida sunshine glinted off the sleek bay colt's well-groomed coat.

Samantha leaned forward to pat Miracle Worker. The black colt snorted and vigorously shook his head. "He feels good today," Samantha commented, taking a firm grip on the reins. Even though the four-year-old colt was a claimer—a horse who ran in the bottom ranks of racing—Samantha wasn't taking any chances on having him run away with her.

Sure enough, Miracle eased down into the slower

trot Samantha had asked him for. "Good boy," she said with satisfaction.

"You behave, too, Gulfstream," her mom said quietly to her mount. Samantha watched as her mother worked to steady Gulfstream Waves. Finally the colt relaxed into a brisk walk. Samantha felt a quick, strong rush of pride as she looked at her mother on the beautiful horse. Gulfstream Waves was the first stakes horse Ian and Suzanne McLean had ever trained. Samantha knew how much he meant to her mother—and to the McLean family's future.

In a week Gulfstream would run in the prestigious Donn Handicap at the Gulfstream Park racetrack, near Miami. Due to Suzanne's excellent exercise-riding and Ian's skillful training the handsome bay colt, with his flashing dark eyes and rippling, bulging muscles, looked every bit the stakes horse now. Samantha could hardly believe he'd ever been just a claimer.

Samantha glanced over at the gap to the track where her dad was watching the exercise session. He waved, and Samantha nodded, but she kept her hands on the reins. *I need to show Dad that I'm a good rider,* she thought. Her dad had just started letting her ride Miracle at the training farm this winter, and only when her mom was around to watch her. Before that, Samantha had been restricted to trail rides on the gentlest horses. Samantha wanted to prove to her dad that his confidence in her was justified.

"Give me a lesson, Mom," she begged.

"Okay, this guy seems to have settled down a bit," Suzanne gave Gulfstream a gentle pat on the shoulder, then she glanced at Samantha.

Aware of her mother's attention, Samantha sat up ramrod straight in the saddle, freezing her hands in what she hoped was the right position over Miracle's neck.

"Relax," her mother said with a laugh. "That's what riding is all about—feeling in tune with your horse. That way you can be ready for whatever he does."

Samantha drew a deep breath and concentrated on the steady four-beat rhythm of Miracle Worker's walk. She could feel herself relaxing. Miracle's ears flicked back, waiting for instructions.

"That's nice. Now pick up a trot," Suzanne instructed.

Samantha clucked and gave a little squeeze with her legs, and Miracle eased into the four beats of the trot. She could feel the power and contained energy of the racehorse beneath her. Breathing deeply to relax, Samantha concentrated on her ride. *This does feel right*, she thought.

"That's it—you're going to be an excellent rider," Suzanne encouraged, the pride in her voice unmistakable. "You've got good hands and a good feel for horses."

Beaming, Samantha slowed Miracle Worker to a walk. "I just want to ride as well as you." Samantha knew that with her red hair and green eyes, she looked like her mother. Now if only she could ride like her . . .

Suzanne smiled. "You will. Just keep at it."

Samantha tucked a few loose strands of her ponytail up under her helmet. "Can we do one little gallop?" she begged.

"Sure—let's gallop them out a couple of furlongs," Suzanne said. "I'll take Gulfstream in the lead, but yell if you feel like you need to stop."

"Okay!" Samantha checked her balance in the saddle, steadied her hands over Miracle's neck, and looked straight ahead, preparing herself for the quick rush of speed to come.

Suzanne moved Gulfstream to the rail and out in front of Miracle Worker. At the signal from his rider, Gulfstream exploded into a gallop. Samantha saw her mom expertly rating him, bringing him down to a slower, more manageable pace.

"Okay, Miracle." Samantha leaned forward. "Go get him!" Miracle shot after Gulfstream, trying to match the stakes horse stride for stride. The two colts ran next to each other for a few seconds before Miracle was forced to drop back.

Glancing ahead, Samantha saw her mother and Gulfstream sweep along the track, a perfect team of energy, motion, and beauty. Samantha quickly checked Miracle's position on the track, keeping him away from the rail, and firmly fixed her gaze on the track ahead of them.

Samantha leaned into the colt's gallop, thrilled to the bones by the quick hammering of his hooves. She forgot that her dad might be watching or that her form might not be quite right. All that mattered was the smooth motion of the racehorse beneath her as she lost herself in his speed.

"Let's pull them up!" her mother called. "That's enough for now."

"Okay!" Samantha caught up with Gulfstream, who Suzanne had already slowed, but the bay colt took off again for a couple of strides. With difficulty Suzanne pulled him back down to a walk. Tossing his head, Gulfstream shied sideways, pretending to be afraid of Miracle.

"That was fun for Miracle," Samantha said, panting from the effort of her ride. She patted the black colt's neck. Miracle wasn't in Gulfstream's class as a racehorse, but Samantha loved him anyway. *I just hope I don't lose him too soon*, she thought with a pang of sadness. Claimers were always for sale. Before any claiming race, a prospective owner could pay a price set on the horses. After the race, no matter who won, the new owner claimed the horse and took it home. Every time Miracle raced, he faced the possibility of going to a new home when the race was done.

"I think we're set for Donn day," Suzanne commented, turning Gulfstream to walk back to the gap. Samantha walked Miracle beside her.

15

Watching Gulfstream step along smartly, bowing his head against Suzanne's restraint, Samantha totally agreed that Gulfstream was ready to run against top competition. *You've come a long way, boy,* she thought.

"Did you ever ride a horse as good as him before?" Samantha asked her mother.

"Not really." Suzanne looked thoughtful. "I haven't really been riding Thoroughbreds for that long. Only since I met your father. When I was growing up, my parents raised Morgans."

Samantha hoped her mom would go on with the story. She had heard about her grandparents' farm many times, but she always liked to hear about it again. Samantha knew that Morgans had a reputation as small, strong horses, with a proud bearing and an alert, intelligent attitude. "When you were my age, your parents had a champion Morgan stallion," she prompted. "And they lived in New England."

"In Vermont," Suzanne replied. "Their prize stallion, Revere's Ride, was said to be almost as great as Justin Morgan, the foundation stallion of the Morgan breed. I'm sorry my parents sold the horses," she added. "I think you'd like riding them. But your grandparents don't have the energy to run a farm anymore."

Samantha nodded. Her grandparents had visited Miami twice, but she didn't feel close to them. They had seemed kind enough but a little stiff. She thought they looked down on her family's lifestyle. Samantha knew that her parents had married very young, and they'd never had much money.

"So Gulfstream is the best horse you've ever ridden?" Samantha asked.

Her mother smiled. "He just might be," she said. "If Gulfstream does well in the Donn, he'll be the best thing that ever happened to us. Your father's reputation will be strong, and we'll be able to make a down payment on our own farm."

Their own farm. Their family would have a real home. Samantha's dad would still be gone a lot—when the meeting at one track ended, he'd still have to travel to another. But Samantha and her mother would be able to stay home in their own house. As things were now, the whole family traveled from track to track. Sam didn't want to complain, but she was tired of living in apartments and house trailers.

"Nice work, you two," Ian greeted Samantha and Suzanne as they approached the gap. Ian had red hair, too, but his was a much darker auburn. A lot of people commented on how colorful the redheaded McLean family was. "Gulfstream's looking fit," Ian added. "We'll van him over to the track in a couple of days."

"The other horses entered in the Donn are already at the track." Samantha swung down off Miracle and grabbed his reins.

"I know, but I want to keep Gulfstream at the

training farm as long as possible," Ian replied. "He's high-strung, even for a Thoroughbred, and it's quieter out here. As a Donn contender, he's going to get a lot of attention once he gets to the track."

"He deserves it!" Samantha said excitedly.

"He sure does," Suzanne agreed.

Samantha turned to hug Gulfstream around the neck—and her fingers met her mom's as Suzanne hugged him from the other side.

"Come here, you two," Ian said, laughing. "Now it's my turn." The McLeans shared a warm hug, with Gulfstream and Miracle Worker looking over their shoulders.

Things are going so well for us, Samantha thought, happily looking up into her parents' loving faces. *And they'll only be better after the Donn!*

After their ride Samantha walked Miracle for half an hour to cool him down, then put him in his stall and brushed him thoroughly. "There you go," she said with satisfaction, stepping back from the colt to admire her work. Miracle's dark coat gleamed like soft licorice. Samantha had treated his black mane and tail with conditioner, and they felt thick and silky to her fingers.

"Maybe you would have been a stakes horse if somebody had treated you right from the beginning," Samantha said. "You sure look like one now."

The colt nosed her affectionately, as if to say thanks for the compliment.

"See you tonight." Samantha closed the stall door and gave him a last pat.

"Let's head back to the trailer and have lunch with your dad," Suzanne called as she walked down the stable aisle. "He's leaving this afternoon for the Fair Grounds track in New Orleans for a couple of days."

Samantha nodded. She knew her dad didn't want to leave Gulfstream so close to the Donn, but he still had obligations to other owners at other tracks.

She stepped outside the barn, sniffing the luscious smell of oranges. Joan and Paul Ivor, who owned the training farm, had planted a grove of oranges behind the barns.

The farm covered over two hundred acres of flat, grassy land. Part of it at the back was swampy, but the level ground was perfect for the training track.

The Ivors, longtime friends of Ian and Suzanne, let Samantha ride on the training track despite her young age. Samantha knew she was incredibly lucky to have the opportunity.

"Ready to go home?" Suzanne jingled her car keys.

"Sure." Samantha walked with her mom to the parking lot where they'd parked their old truck.

The McLeans' house trailer was only a short distance from the track. Samantha thought it was the nicest place they'd lived so far. The outside of the trailer was painted a bright white, and her mom had painted the trim palm tree green and had planted brightly colored tropical flowers out front.

"It'll be sad to leave here," Samantha said. "But I can't wait till we get our farm."

"Well, the Maguire place is a real possibility." Suzanne looked thoughtful. "We'd have enough to cover the down payment, and they've got foaling facilities as well as a training barn and track."

"Oooh, we'd have our own babies!" Samantha danced up the steps to the trailer, picturing the foals frolicking in the Florida sunshine.

"Not right away," Suzanne cautioned. "We'd have to build up to that." She stepped from the living room into the tiny kitchen.

"Hi, sweetheart," Ian greeted Suzanne, turning from the kitchen cupboard. "I picked up everything on your list."

"Good—that's our survival food for when you're gone." Suzanne winked at Samantha, and Samantha smiled. *I'll miss Dad, but Mom and I are going to have fun!* she thought.

"What's for lunch?" she asked.

"Linguini with clam sauce." Suzanne filled a pot with water. "I've got the sauce already made."

"I'll help you," Samantha volunteered, carefully slicing the loaf of Italian bread on the counter. She thought it would be fun to know how to cook as well as her mom.

"So what are you two going to do while I'm gone?" Ian asked as they sat down to lunch.

Suzanne passed him the bread. "Work with the horses. And, you know, girl things."

"Girl things, eh? Sounds mysterious," Ian said, smiling.

I wonder what Mom's got in mind? Samantha thought, twirling her linguini around a fork. *Maybe she'll let me dye my hair!*

After lunch Ian carried his suitcase to the door. "I'll see you on Thursday," he said.

"Take care of yourself," Suzanne said firmly, reaching up to put her hands on Ian's shoulders. Ian bent to give her a long, romantic kiss.

Ian closed the door, and Suzanne turned to Samantha with a grin that made Samantha feel like her mother was her age. "What should we do first?" Samantha asked.

"The dishes!" her mother joked. "What did you want to do?"

"Give me a makeover!" Samantha pleaded. Her father always teased her when she curled her hair or wore makeup. But Samantha loved her mother's attention—and how much older she looked afterward.

Suzanne gestured grandly at the bathroom. "Madame, I believe you have the next appointment," she said.

Samantha sat next to the sink on a chair with a

21

plastic seat. "Let's do your hair first," Suzanne suggested, reaching under the sink for the hot rollers. She began to brush Samantha's hair, and Samantha leaned into the long, relaxing strokes.

"Can we dye my hair blond?" she asked.

Suzanne stopped brushing and stared at her in the mirror. "Samantha! Most people would kill to have hair the color of yours. It's absolutely beautiful."

"But everybody notices it," Samantha protested. "I want to fit in."

"Someday you'll be glad that people notice you." Suzanne resumed brushing. "You're very special."

Suzanne washed Samantha's hair in the sink, then put it up in big rollers. Samantha looked in the mirror and giggled. "Dad would really tease me if he saw me like this," she said.

"Your dad thinks you're perfect just the way you are," Suzanne said, carefully smoothing on a facial mask. "And he's right. You're a natural beauty, Samantha. But this is fun."

Samantha beamed. When she was with her mom, she really could believe that she was beautiful. Other times Samantha felt uncertain about her looks. In the past year she had shot up to five-foot four, and she was very thin. She was sure the light dusting of freckles across her nose didn't help her appearance, either.

Her mom began removing the hot rollers. She carefully balanced them on the edge of the sink. "When we get our own place, we'll have a huge bathroom, with tons of room for makeovers," she declared.

"I really liked the house at the Maguire place," Samantha said. "Did you, Mom?"

"Yes." Suzanne fanned the dryer over Samantha's head. "The big kitchen and living room are wonderful."

"And I loved 'my' room there." Samantha remembered the pillow-covered window seat and the giant bay windows with their view of the back pastures of the farm. "But I'll go anywhere," she added.

Suzanne laughed. "Anywhere?"

"It'd be so much fun to have a real home and just stay in one place," Samantha said.

Suzanne cupped Samantha's face in her hands. "We do have a real home, honey. It's not the place that matters—it's the three of us together as a family."

"I know." Samantha smiled brightly. "But I still can't wait until Gulfstream wins the Donn!"

"Samantha, you know Gulfstream may not win," Suzanne cautioned.

"I know, but if he does . . ." Samantha narrowed her green eyes as her mom peeled away the facial mask. Suzanne's expression was eager and excited. "You hope he wins just as much as I do!" Samantha said.

"Of course." Suzanne laughed. "I've got more dreams than I can count."

"So what will our horses be like?" Samantha asked, wanting to continue their shared fantasy.

Suzanne laughed. "Well, since we're dreaming here, I guess we'll have at least one Triple Crown winner."

Samantha imagined what it would be like to own a horse who could win the three greatest races in the country.

"And, of course, just for the scenery, we'll have a horse of every color." Suzanne capped the mascara. "There—you're done. And you look sensational, if I do say so myself."

Samantha looked into the mirror. She saw a glamorous young woman, maybe sixteen years old, with a headful of shimmering red waves, brilliant green eyes fringed by dark lashes, and a smooth, flawless complexion. She smiled, admiring how white her teeth looked against her peach-colored lip gloss. "Cool!" she said. "Thanks, Mom!"

"You're welcome." Suzanne smiled back. "That was a labor of love. Now I'd better get some work done—I need to go over our finances."

That won't be a worry when Gulfstream wins, Samantha thought as she wandered into her bedroom. The room was tiny, holding only Samantha's antique walnut bed, a movable clothes rack, and a bureau. Three framed pictures of great racehorses—Secretariat, Ruffian, and Bold Ruler—hung on the walls. The window looked out on the driveway.

Maybe her mom and dad would even have another baby if they had more money. Samantha had always wanted a brother or sister—especially a sister—to share secrets and fun with.

Samantha sat down on her bed and smiled into the mirror over her bureau. *Only a little while longer,* she thought. *And then all our dreams will come true.*

2

"HAVE FUN AT THE BEACH," SUZANNE SAID, LOOKING UP from the stack of ledgers piled on the kitchen table.

"I will!" Samantha said. "Are you sure you don't want to come?"

Her mother looked at the piles of paper and made a face. "I don't think I'm going anywhere today. You and Tiffany get some sun for me."

Samantha gave her mother a kiss and let herself out the door to the trailer. She stopped to check her beach bag one last time: a towel, sunscreen, lip balm, the latest issue of *Seventeen* magazine. Yep, she had everything she needed. Her best friend, Tiffany Rivera, was meeting her at the beach, which was only a five-minute walk from Samantha's home.

I definitely look good enough for the beach today, Samantha thought as she hurried across the palm-lined street in front of the trailer park. Miami Beach, near the Gulfstream racetrack, was home to movie stars and other wealthy people. *Maybe I'll see somebody famous today!* Samantha grinned. *On the other hand, I look so glamorous, maybe everyone will think I'm famous.*

Samantha crossed the park in front of the beach. She could already hear the cries of children playing on the sand and the loud cawing of seagulls. The smell of hamburgers and French fries wafted to her from the pier.

The beach, a smooth, inviting expanse of satiny white sand, bordered the blue-green, tropical water of the Atlantic Ocean. Blankets and umbrellas dotted the sand with bright splashes of color.

"Sammy, over here!" Tiffany was waving from her beach blanket near the water.

Samantha waved back, but she ran down to the water before joining her friend. Gentle waves broke on the beach, and the water lapped at her feet, filling her footprints before retreating out to sea.

Samantha waded into the ocean, enjoying the cool water on her legs, then turned and walked up the beach to join Tiffany. She set her beach bag on Tiffany's blanket and dropped down beside her.

Tiffany gazed at her, then snatched off her mirrored sunglasses. "Wow, Sammy—you look fantastic!"

"Thanks. One of my mom's makeovers," Samantha

explained, glancing at her friend. As always, Tiffany looked great. With her sun-streaked chestnut hair, dark blue eyes, and mischievous dimples, Tiffany was one of the most popular girls in the seventh grade.

"Well, she went all out this time." Tiffany grinned.

"I know, I know—I don't usually look this good," Samantha joked.

"You're usually too busy with horses to care." Tiffany put her sunglasses back on and gazed out over the beach.

Samantha smiled at her friend and slipped out of her cutoffs and T-shirt, revealing her green one-piece bathing suit underneath. Tiffany rode sometimes with Samantha, but she wasn't really into horses. She was a cheerleader and on the student council. Samantha knew she was better with horses than Tiffany, but her friend was much better with people.

Samantha pulled her sunblock out of her tote bag and slathered it on her arms, neck, and face. Leaning back on her elbows on the blanket, she scanned the shoreline. Down near the water a group of boys had set up a volleyball net and were choosing sides. "It's not really crowded today," she commented.

Tiffany grasped Samantha's arm and and sat up straighter. "Sammy, look! Here come Jason and Nick!"

"Where?" Samantha tried to look cool. Jason Renz and Nick Hartman were the two cutest guys in her class.

"Hey, Sammy." Jason smiled down at her. His

longish hair was streaked with blond from the sun, and his bright aqua bathing trunks showed off his golden tan. He bounced a volleyball from hand to hand.

"What's goin' on?" Nick asked.

"Not much, as you can see," Tiffany replied, pushing her hair behind her shoulders. "Just relaxing, hanging out."

Jason twirled the volleyball on his finger. "Want to watch us play?" he asked.

Samantha grinned at Tiffany. "Sure," she said.

"The view is good from here," Tiffany agreed.

"Cool." Jason and Nick walked off, tossing the volleyball to each other.

Tiffany slid her sunglasses down her nose and winked at Samantha. "They can play as long as they like," she said.

"Won't hurt my eyes," Samantha agreed. Samantha slipped on her sunglasses to watch the game. The boys quickly picked sides, then began a fast-paced volley. Jason dove into the sand for the ball, hitting it high into the air with his fists. Then Nick slammed it over the net to score a point. The two exchanged a high five.

Samantha tipped her face up to the sun, soaking in the bright, strong rays. The ocean waves pounded rhythmically against the shore, dissolving in white foam on the beach and lulling her into hazy contentment.

"This is my second favorite way to spend the afternoon," she declared.

"Yeah, if only we had a couple of horses out here, it would be perfect," Tiffany teased her friend. She knew that Samantha would rather be at the barn than anywhere else—no matter how nice the day was. Tiffany brushed sand off her legs and frowned. "But tomorrow we have school, and we get back our history tests—what a drag."

"I'm sure you did okay," Samantha said. She'd never admit it, but Samantha actually liked school, especially English, and she'd never had a hard time making good grades.

"I'll bet you aced the history test." Tiffany sighed and looked back at the volleyball game. "I wish some of your smartness would rub off on me."

"You're smart enough," Samantha said quickly.

"Tell that to my parents." Tiffany sat forward and cupped her face in her hands. "Boy, look at Jason and Nick go. This is what I call live entertainment."

"I'm not a bit bored," Samantha agreed.

Jason said something to Nick and his other teammates. A moment later he jogged over toward the girls' blanket.

"How'd you like the game?" Jason asked, pushing damp hair off his forehead.

"You're really good," Samantha answered. She felt flustered by all of Jason's attention but thrilled, too.

Jason shrugged. "Yeah, well, I play all the time. So, I guess I'll see you at school tomorrow?"

"I guess." Samantha hoped Jason would think it was sunburn that was making her turn beet red.

"Okay, so—catch you later." Jason ran back to his game.

Tiffany was grinning from ear to ear. "Jason really likes you, Sammy."

"Do you think?" Samantha could feel she was still blushing.

"For sure." Tiffany stretched and began to gather her things. "I've got to help my mom," she said reluctantly. Tiffany's mom ran a flower shop in town. Tiffany began to stuff her towel and other beach things into her beach bag. "You can give me back the blanket later."

"Take it—I think I'll go for a walk or a swim."

"Okay. See you at school." Tiffany slung her bag over her shoulder and headed across the beach.

Samantha got up and walked to the edge of the water, her toes sinking deep into the grainy, damp sand. She kept going until the water was waist high, then plunged into the waves.

The water was warm and salty. Samantha swam for a while with steady, practiced strokes, then dove under. Swimming through the silent, blue-green water, she pretended she was a mermaid.

At last Samantha broke the surface of the water, gasping for breath. She sloshed to the shore, the tide tugging at her feet.

A stiff ocean breeze cooled her as she walked

along the beach. Samantha ruffled her hair with her hand and breathed deeply, inhaling the fresh, salty air.

She stopped to let a pair of handsome, bold seagulls march across the beach in front of her. The lively black-and-white birds flapped their wings and began brazenly begging from a group of picnickers.

Samantha laughed out loud. *I love walking on the beach*, she thought. Shading her eyes with her hand, Samantha gazed out to sea, letting her thoughts roam with the sailboats and fishing boats that bobbed far out on the horizon.

"I hope Gulfstream wins the Donn and we can stay in Miami Beach for good," Samantha murmured. *I promise never to ask for anything again in my life.*

When Samantha got home, her mother was waiting for her. They went straight down to the training barn for the evening chores. "I'll start feeding at this end of the barn, and you start at that end," Suzanne said. She had already measured out into buckets the mixture of grain, vitamins, and minerals for the seven horses Ian trained.

"Okay." Samantha picked up two buckets and headed for the stalls of Rival Claim and Gone by Day, two five-year-old mares her father had recently added to his string.

Rival Claim, a black mare with a jagged, lightning-shaped blaze, was pawing impatiently in her stall. "You're feeling better," Samantha said as she unhooked the netting at the front of the stall and stepped inside. Rival Claim had torn a muscle in her shoulder before Ian bought her for a new owner. Most people on the backside thought she would never run again, but Samantha knew her dad was almost sure he could bring the mare back up to form.

Rival Claim eagerly pushed her muzzle into her grain. "You've got a good appetite," Samantha said approvingly. "I bet you'll be out on the track again in no time."

Gone by Day waited at the front of her stall, ears laid back. "Hey, don't bite me!" Samantha warned, pouring Gone by Day's feed as fast as she could. The ornery bay mare seemed to be thinking about nipping her, but Samantha was out of the stall before she could try it.

Not all the claimers have great personalities, Samantha thought ruefully as she shut the door. Who knew how many bad owners and aches and pains Gone by Day had suffered through?

"Sunburst's not nasty, though—and she's had the hardest life of all, I bet," Samantha murmured, heading eagerly for the stall of Marcy's Sunburst. Next to Gulfstream and Miracle, Sunburst was her favorite horse of all.

"Here I come, girl!" Samantha called. Sunburst was in a stall at the very end of the row.

The old claimer stuck her head out of the stall at the sound of Samantha's voice and whinnied softly.

Samantha poured Sunburst's grain into her tray, then carried a bucket of grooming tools into the stall. She began to brush the mare's rough brown coat.

"You really don't look so bad," Samantha murmured. She knew her father considered Sunburst the worst off of all the claimers he trained. Sunburst was old for a racehorse—nearly seven—and she had suffered bone chips in her knees and an abscess in one of her front hooves. Samantha's heart had gone out to the sweet older horse, who waited so patiently in her stall. When Sunburst had arrived at the training farm two weeks ago, she didn't seem to expect much out of life.

Sunburst finished the last of her grain and looked around at Samantha. "Let's brush your face," Samantha said, rubbing the dandy brush gently down the mare's forehead. "I'm going to make you beautiful." Samantha brushed out the mare's mane and tail, then stepped back to check her work.

Samantha knew that Sunburst had never had perfect conformation. Her neck was a little thick, and she was over a bit at the knees—her legs weren't as straight as they should be. But her coat gleamed with health and from the daily brushings, and her eyes were bright. "You look just gorgeous," Samantha said, hugging the mare gently around the neck. "You'll win a few more races, then you'll go to a good home as a pleasure horse. Somebody's sure to want a horse as nice as you."

Sunburst nickered as if she was grateful for the praise. Samantha let herself out of the stall, then slowly walked down the barn aisle, looking at her dad's claimers. They all had health or training problems that Ian had either solved or was working on.

Training claimers is hard, Samantha thought. *It would be easier just to get good young horses to train— ones that nobody's hurt.*

She stopped at Gulfstream's stall, praying that he was all right. Gulfstream had been healthy when the McLeans had taken over his care, but they didn't know much about most of his life as a claimer.

The big bay colt stood quietly at the back of his stall, watching Samantha with his dark eyes.

"What are you thinking?" Samantha asked, stretching a hand over the netting. "Are you going to win big on Saturday?"

The colt continued to watch her, but he stayed at the back of his stall. He'd never been too friendly. Samantha supposed that people had been unkind to him in the past, and now he had trouble trusting anyone.

"Hello, Samantha." A gray-haired man was walking briskly toward her. "How's Gulfstream doing?"

Samantha recognized Richard Stockton, one of the leading trainers at the track. "Hello, Mr. Stockton," she replied. "Gulfstream's just fine." Samantha was surprised Mr. Stockton even knew who she was. *I guess everybody knows me now that my dad has a horse running in the Donn!* she thought proudly.

"Hey, Sammy." Rob Benson, Gulfstream's jockey, joined her in front of Gulfstream's stall. The slight, dark-haired young man nodded at the colt. "The farrier's coming in a minute—I think one of Gulfstream's front shoes is a little loose."

"It's a good thing you noticed," Samantha said, glancing down at the horse's feet. She knew that even the slightest shoeing problem could cause a horse to pull up lame in a race. Rob was one of the top jockeys in the country, and he was very careful with his mounts. "Do you think he's ready otherwise?" she asked eagerly.

"I've been thinking about that," Rob said seriously. "I've been spending time with him, trying to get inside his head. Horse psychology is important in a race."

"So what did you find out?" Samantha wondered what Rob would say. She didn't think she understood Gulfstream very well. Her mom understood him the best of anyone, but Gulfstream acted strangely sometimes even with her.

Rob frowned. "Not all that much," he said. "He's hard to read. He throws his heart into running, but I'm not always sure he wants to beat the other horses. He just runs because that's what he was bred to do."

"Do you think he'll be all right on Saturday?"

Samantha asked quietly, but her voice trembled. So much depended on the race.

"I think so." Rob nodded. "He's very strong. He's just unpredictable."

"Okay, I'm ready for him," called Donny Zamora, the farrier. He walked into Gulfstream's stall, wiping his hands on the heavy leather chaps he wore for shoeing.

Gulfstream pranced out of the stall behind Donny, tossing his head and skittering in a spirited way. Just looking at him, Samantha felt all her doubts evaporate.

"You're going to be famous, boy," she said firmly. "I just know it. I can't wait for race day."

3

THE AFTERNOON OF THE DONN HANDICAP, SAMANTHA stood beside her parents and Gulfstream in the saddling paddock at the track. Taking a deep breath, she handed her father the colt's tiny racing saddle. "This is it," she said.

Ian took the saddle. "Nervous?" he asked, flipping it over Gulfstream's back.

Samantha shook her head. "Not really." She thought that Gulfstream couldn't look better. His gleaming, healthy bay coat was the color of caramel, and his slender black legs were straight and powerful. Samantha thought he was the most impressive horse in the field. The other spectators must have thought so, too. Gulfstream was going into the race as the favorite.

The bay colt shivered as Ian tightened the girth on the saddle. Suzanne held Gulfstream's reins tight and rubbed his nose. "I'm not nervous, either," she said. "But I am excited!"

"Me too!" Samantha forced herself to stand still. She didn't want to telegraph her nervous excitement to Gulfstream.

"He's ready," Ian said.

The bay colt tossed his head and stared out at the crowds of people bustling in front of the saddling paddock.

Samantha followed his gaze. "I wonder what he thinks about all this."

"He's raced for years—he knows what's coming," Suzanne said.

The day was hot and bright, with clean-edged, puffy white clouds in a flawless blue sky. *Gulfstream's a Florida-bred horse, and this is his home,* Samantha thought, squinting in the strong sunlight. *He should win it today!* Over half of the nine-horse field in the Donn were from out of state.

"Here come the Quinns," Ian said. Samantha knew that her dad enjoyed training for Gulfstream's owners. They were interested in his work with the colt, but they didn't try to do Ian's job for him.

"How's he doing?" asked Mr. Quinn, stepping into Gulfstream's open-ended stall. Mr. Quinn was a tall man in his sixties. His wife and grown daughter, Margaret, crowded into the stall behind him. Gulfstream began to shift his weight nervously from leg to leg.

Samantha saw a look of alarm cross her dad's face. Too many people were pushing around an excitable racehorse. "Why don't you all step outside the stall?" Ian asked, ushering the Quinns backward while Suzanne held Gulfstream.

Mrs. Quinn smiled. "That's Ian's nice way of telling us we're in the way, dear," she said to her husband.

"Well, I've seen what I want to see," Mr. Quinn declared. "He looks good, Ian."

"We'll be standing in the winner's circle," said Margaret.

"I hope so." Ian waved to the Quinns as they walked to the stands.

Samantha couldn't help comparing her jeans, T-shirt with the racetrack logo, and boots to the two women's flowered, elegant, cotton dresses and strappy sandals. "I wish I'd had time to change," she said to her mom.

Suzanne laughed. "Sweetie, you and I are exercise riders! We've done our best for Gulfstream—we should be proud of our work clothes."

Gulfstream snorted sharply. "He's saying it's time to go," Samantha said. She felt a rush of butterflies in her stomach.

"Okay, let's get him to the walking ring." Ian stepped out of the stall. Suzanne gave a firm nod. Between them they led Gulfstream the short distance to the grass-bordered walking ring.

Samantha was careful to stay out of the way. She slipped under the rail bordering the saddling paddock and joined the rest of the spectators surging to get a look at their favorite horses.

She spotted the green-and-white racing silks of the Quinns' Three Willow farm and made her way around the rail to where Rob Benson stood waiting for Gulfstream. "How's it going, Sammy?" he asked as she slipped under the rail next to him, but the young jockey's eyes were on Gulfstream.

"Okay." Samantha watched Gulfstream, too. The colt danced along behind Ian and Suzanne, but he was minding. Samantha noted that Gulfstream's head was a little less refined than the heads of the other horses pacing around the walking ring, and his conformation was blockier. But the perfectly conditioned muscles on his neck, shoulders, and hindquarters showed his strength.

"He should be up for this," Rob said. "Last Wednesday, I drilled him four furlongs."

"He is!" Samantha smiled as her parents led Gulfstream over to them. She checked the odds board. "He's still going in as the favorite, and he's going to win this race!"

Ian gave Rob a leg into the saddle. "Let Gulfstream find his footing and settle, then go with him," he instructed. "He tends to panic unless he can get his bearings."

"Okay." Rob was all business. "I won't go for the lead right away unless I'm being left in the dust."

"The rain this week should help," Suzanne said.

"Gulfstream likes a track with a little give to it." Rob nodded.

Ian let go of Gulfstream's bridle. "Good luck."

"Thanks." Rob gathered his reins and pointed Gulfstream toward the hedge-lined tunnel to the track.

"Let's go up to the stands." Suzanne took Samantha's hand. "I think you might be right, Samantha—we're going to win this race," she said as they walked to their seats.

Samantha could see from her dad's tense face that he wasn't nearly as sure.

Samantha shook her head. She knew she shouldn't count on Gulfstream winning, but it seemed to her like the most important thing in the world. So much depended on this race—her dad's career, her family's home . . .

Suzanne squeezed Samantha's hand. "We've done all we could, and he's a wonderful horse," she said, seeming to read Samantha's mind.

"I know." Samantha took a deep breath, trying to calm her nerves. She wiped her sweaty hands on the legs of her jeans and took a seat in the stands with her parents.

"There's Gulfstream!" Suzanne pointed at the track. Rob was trotting the colt counterclockwise toward the starting gate.

"Gulfstream's really wired," Samantha said anxiously. The colt was pulling hard on the reins and leaning in sideways, drifting toward the rail. "Do you think he'll use himself up before the race?"

"No, he should have plenty left. I've trained him for that." Ian trained his binoculars on the field. "The horses are going to post now."

Samantha slid to the edge of her seat as she watched the assistant starter guide Gulfstream into the number-five slot of the gate. "He's settling down," she said with relief.

"He's always been good in the gate," Suzanne muttered.

Samantha noticed that the faint lines around her mother's mouth were more pronounced than usual as she bit her lips. *Mom's really nervous about the race, too—no matter what she says*, Samantha thought. She shaded her eyes and fixed her gaze on Gulfstream. She knew the break from the gate would be important, and she didn't want to miss a thing.

"The horses are in the gate," the announcer called as the last horse loaded. "And they're off!"

The horses burst from the gate, soaring high in the air. The next instant they crashed to the ground, digging for footing in the soft, sandy dirt of the track.

"Go, Gulfstream!" Samantha screamed. *Oh, please, please do well*, she begged silently as she crossed her fingers. As the horses roared by the stands for the first time, Samantha quickly searched for the green and white of Rob's racing silks. In a few moments she spotted him. "Oh, no!" she cried. Gulfstream was dead last in the field of nine—and the field was pulling away!

"Easily Done grabs a short lead as they come into the first turn," the announcer called. "Back one length to Fine by Me. Jewel of Eire is running in third."

Glancing distractedly up the track, Samantha saw that Easily Done, a big dapple gray colt and the record holder of the NYRA Mile at the Aqueduct track last fall, had increased his lead to three lengths. Fine by Me and Jewel of Eire, both chestnut colts, were battling for second. But Gulfstream was still last. He wasn't losing ground, but he wasn't gaining, either, as the field plunged around the first turn into the backstretch.

"Dad, what's happening to Gulfstream?" Samantha almost sobbed. "He's out of the race!"

"No, he isn't—not yet!" Ian didn't look away from the track, but his hands were white as he gripped his binoculars.

"Secretariat almost always ran last in the first part of his races," Suzanne said quickly, referring to one of the greatest racehorses of all time.

But Gulfstream isn't Secretariat—he's just a former claimer! Samantha dropped her head in her hands, despair making her feel sick. She couldn't stand to watch. Why had she pinned all her hopes on Gulfstream?

"Gulfstream Waves trails the field," the announcer

called. "But wait! He's digging in deep! Rob Benson is taking him between horses—Gulfstream Waves moves into fifth, no, fourth! And they're coming into the stretch!"

Samantha could see that Easily Done and Jewel of Eire were tiring. Slowly, steadily Gulfstream was eating into their lead. He was around Jewel of Eire on the inside as the other colt drifted wide from the rail. He had passed Fine by Me. Now only Easily Done remained between Gulfstream and victory!

"Run, Gulfstream!" Samantha screamed. But Easily Done wasn't fading. He had a two-length lead over Gulfstream with only a furlong to go!

"Give it all you've got, boy!" Suzanne yelled. Her voice sounded so much like Samantha's, for an instant Samantha thought she'd spoken herself.

Suddenly Easily Done began backing up—slowing so fast, he almost seemed to be moving backward. "He was only good for a mile, like in the NYRA Mile," Ian sputtered. "He doesn't have enough!"

"Gulfstream Waves takes the lead!" the announcer cried. "He's pulling away from Easily Done. There he goes!"

"Yes!" Samantha screamed. "Go, Gulfstream—you're winning!"

Gulfstream's powerful strides never wavered. Seconds later he swept under the wire, the winner by four lengths.

"Look at the board," Samantha gasped, pointing to

the large neon odds board, which showed the fractions, or how fast each quarter mile of the race had been run. "That's the fastest Gulfstream's ever run! Oh, Mom, Dad! Let's go to him!"

"You bet!" Ian looked dazed but happy.

Suzanne gripped Samantha's hands. "Samantha, can you believe it?"

"Yes!" Samantha smiled deeply into her mother's green eyes. Samantha saw her own joy and relief mirrored there.

"Come on!" Ian quickly led the way out of the stands.

Rob had ridden Gulfstream back to the gap. The colt's neck was lathered with sweat, and he was snorting and shying from the crowd. "Stand clear," Rob warned.

Suzanne stepped forward and gripped Gulfstream's reins. "I've got him."

"Thanks." Rob jumped down.

Samantha gave the horse a hard, fast hug as tears of joy streamed down her cheeks. "Oh, Gulfstream, you're the best!" she cried.

Gulfstream touched his nose briefly to her hair, then jerked his head away.

"Watch out, Samantha," Suzanne said. "He's pretty excited."

Samantha quickly stepped back. Suzanne firmly rubbed Gulfstream's neck, and the colt's eyes stopped rolling. *He's always been Mom's horse,* Samantha thought as the press crowded in with their cameras. *But right now the world thinks he belongs to them!*

"Let's get him to the winner's circle," Ian said. Samantha had never seen her dad look so thrilled. "Then we're going to celebrate at the best restaurant in town!"

"Sounds wonderful, doesn't it, Samantha?" Suzanne asked, her voice quivering. "Don't cry!" she added, wiping her eyes.

"You are!" Samantha hardly ever saw her mother cry. *This race meant everything to her, too,* Samantha realized.

Suzanne led Gulfstream to the winner's circle and posed him in front of the border of red and white tulips. She held Gulfstream's reins while Ian, Samantha, Rob, and the Quinns crowded around for the winner's photos.

Wiping away her tears of joy, Samantha beamed into the cameras. *My life is so great,* she thought as the cameras clicked.

4

"FINALLY, A QUIET DAY," SAMANTHA SAID TO HER MOM. Samantha blew out a deep, relaxing breath and eased her grip on Miracle's reins a notch.

Suzanne rode just in front of her, exercising Gulfstream for the first time since the Donn. Samantha was keeping them company and tuning up Miracle for his next claiming race in two days.

The day after the race Ian had sent Gulfstream back to the training farm to rest. The excitable colt had been too upset to eat the first night. He was still off his feed.

"It's nice to be alone, isn't it?" Samantha called to her mom.

"The last few days have been pretty hectic," Suzanne agreed.

Gulfstream's come-from-behind win had instantly

captured the interest of the track reporters. They'd made much of his rags-to-riches story—from claimer to grade-one stakes winner—and of Ian McLean as a rising young star in the Thoroughbred training world. But finally the uproar over the Cinderella-like winner of the Donn had died down. Samantha was glad life was getting back to normal.

Samantha clucked to Miracle, encouraging the black colt to catch up to Gulfstream. But the big bay racehorse wouldn't permit it. As Miracle's head drew even with his flank, Gulfstream broke into a high-stepping trot, hauling on the reins.

"What's wrong with him?" Samantha called. "He's been acting all weird since the race."

"Oh, I think the attention bothered him." Suzanne shrugged. "He'll settle down in a minute, when he sees it's just us out here."

Samantha pulled Miracle Worker back behind Gulfstream, but the bay colt was still jerking his head with every stride. "Why doesn't he like attention?" she asked. Most racehorses she'd seen loved it. They all seemed to know when they'd won. Some of them even seemed to pose for the cameras.

"I think he has bad memories of racing, winner's circles, and crowds," Suzanne said sympathetically. "Every time the poor guy won when he was a claimer, it just meant he had to run again—probably before he was rested." She lightly patted the bay colt's neck as Gulfstream finally settled into a spirited trot.

Samantha sat back in Miracle's saddle with a contented sigh. *She* had certainly enjoyed all the attention from Gulfstream's win. That night the McLeans had gone to one of Miami's fanciest seafood restaurants. Samantha had filled up on fresh lobster, one of her favorite foods, while her father and mother talked nonstop about the race and the farm they'd buy.

The celebration hadn't stopped there. After dinner the Quinns had thrown a lavish party for the McLeans, themselves, and what seemed to Samantha like half of Miami. Wearing a beautiful dress bought hastily for the occasion, with her hair up, Samantha had felt like high society. The party had lasted most of the night.

That was fun, but it really is nice that things are back to normal, she thought, cautiously moving Miracle up on Gulfstream again. For the moment the high-strung colt seemed to tolerate it.

Samantha sniffed. The late morning air smelled faintly of an approaching storm and the day was cloudy and a little cool. *No beach later today,* she thought. Samantha felt a pang of disappointment. *That means no volleyball players, either.*

"What are you thinking about?" Suzanne asked.

"Oh, just stuff," Samantha tried to say it casually, but she was blushing as if her mother had read her mind.

Suzanne smiled. "Well, it must be interesting 'stuff,'" she teased. "Your face is as red as my hair!"

Samantha quickly snapped back to the present as Miracle stumbled on an uneven place on the track. *Don't forget what you're doing,* she reminded herself.

Samantha glanced quickly around the track. While she'd been daydreaming, two other exercise riders had ridden onto the track. They must have finished their warm-ups and were galloping their horses slowly along the backstretch. Samantha recognized Rob Benson on one of the horses, a good-looking three-year-old entered next month in the Florida Derby.

"How's Gulfstream doing?" Samantha asked her mom.

"Pretty well—I don't think he's sore from the race," Suzanne replied. "But I feel like I'm sitting on a powder keg."

Samantha looked closely at Gulfstream. The colt was shaking his head, and his neck, arched as he fought Suzanne's restraint, was lathered despite the cool day. His luxuriant black tail streamed out behind him.

He looks so pretty, Samantha thought. "What are you going to do with him, Mom?" she asked.

"Go on ahead," Suzanne instructed. Her expression was intent as she struggled with Gulfstream. "Let me work with him by himself for a minute."

Samantha trotted Miracle on a few paces around the turn and looked back. Gulfstream was yanking on the reins, dragging Suzanne to the inside of the track, where the horses moved at faster paces.

With a quick feeling of dread, Samantha saw that the other two horses on the track were rapidly galloping toward them. She could tell from the steady increase in the staccato of their hooves that they would start breezing as they came off the far turn, moving into full racing gear. "Mom, watch out!" Samantha pointed at the other horses.

"I see them," Suzanne gasped. As if he had, too, Gulfstream exploded into a gallop. Suzanne pulled him down hard into a trot, but he was still drifting toward the inside lane.

"The other horses aren't stopping!" Samantha cried. They had begun their breeze at the three-eighths pole and were pounding down the stretch. *Those riders can't see Gulfstream acting up around the turn*, Samantha thought, her fear mounting. *They'll run into him!*

"Come on, Miracle," she said quickly. "We've got to help Gulfstream!"

Samantha's thoughts were a blur. What should she do? There was no time to ask her mom. Could she ride up next to Gulfstream and grab his reins like a pony rider at the track? She began to ride Miracle back toward the bay colt. Suddenly Gulfstream exploded straight up in the air and came down in a flat-out racing gallop.

Samantha watched as her mother struggled to

regain her seat. She could see that Gulfstream was running out of control. *You've got to do something*, Samantha ordered herself. *But what?* Maybe Miracle could block Gulfstream! Samantha stopped Miracle, then frantically cued him with her right heel to move sideways. She had no idea if he would respond— Miracle was a racehorse, not a reining horse.

But the black colt obediently wheeled to stand at a right angle to the track. Samantha let out a shuddering gasp of relief. Gulfstream was coming up on them fast.

"Maybe Gulfstream will want to stand with you," Samantha whispered. Gulfstream was so close, she could see the whites of his rolling eyes and the red of his flared nostrils. "Except he doesn't like other horses ahead of him. . . . Oh, no! This is wrong—he won't stop!"

Hauling on the reins, Samantha tried to wrench Miracle out of Gulfstream's way. But the claimer wouldn't turn to the right. Gulfstream was just strides away!

Frozen with terror, Samantha stared as Gulfstream came closer and closer. *He's going to run right over us!* she thought, bracing herself for the impact.

Suzanne's eyes were narrowed with concentration as she repeatedly yanked on Gulfstream's reins, trying to slow him. But the out-of-control colt didn't respond. He continued his headlong rush at Miracle and Samantha.

More frightened than she'd ever been in her life, Samantha frantically tried to urge Miracle to back up. As if he had realized the danger they were in, Miracle began trying to back away, but Samantha knew they'd never make it in time. Gulfstream was almost on top of them at full racing speed.

In that last moment Suzanne looked at Samantha with the same concentrated, intent gaze she had just given Gulfstream. Then she pulled the colt hard toward the inside.

To Samantha's amazement, Gulfstream responded for the first time. Perfectly together, he and Suzanne headed straight for the rail.

"No!" Samantha cried. *"No!"*

Horse and rider crashed through the rail with a sickening splintering noise. Suzanne was thrown over Gulfstream's head. She tumbled to the ground and didn't move.

"Mom!" Samantha screamed, flinging herself out of the saddle and running to her mother. Miracle galloped off around the track in fright. "Are you okay?"

Suzanne lay on her back. Her lovely face was pale, and she had a cut on her forehead. *She's hurt,* Samantha thought, kneeling by her mother's side. *She'd have to be after a fall like that!* "Help!" Samantha cried. Gulfstream lay on the grass nearby, groaning and struggling to rise. Samantha gripped her ears, trying to block out the sound.

"Sammy!" It was her dad's voice. She didn't know

where he had come from. He pulled her to her feet. "Stay with me. The ambulance is coming."

"The doctors will help Mom." Samantha's teeth were chattering. Suzanne would go to the hospital, then be fine. She'd been in the hospital before, with a broken leg. She'd been in a lot of pain, but that night Samantha and her dad had gone to see her and joked about the bad hospital food.

Samantha knew this had been a bad fall. *Mom will be fine,* she told herself again. *She'll be fine.*

The ambulance pulled up, and the EMTs gathered around Suzanne. They quickly conferred, then loaded her onto a stretcher. One of the EMTs tripped as they walked quickly to the ambulance, jerking his corner of the stretcher.

"Be careful, you'll hurt her!" Samantha screamed.

"Sammy, they're not—," her father began, but Samantha had broken free of his grip and run to the side of the stretcher.

"I'm here, Mom," she whispered. "Don't worry."

Suzanne's face was quiet and tranquil, as if she understood. Samantha softly touched her mother's cheek. *Why is she still unconscious? They have to hurry and get her to the hospital!*

Ian gripped Samantha's shoulders hard as the stretcher was loaded into the ambulance.

"I want to ride with Mom to the hospital," Samantha whispered. The blood roaring in her ears made it hard for her to hear.

Ian's face was white and frightened. "I don't think that would be a good idea, Sammy."

The EMTs banged shut the ambulance doors. "Don't leave," Samantha cried. "Please!"

"Wait here with Rob," Ian said. His voice was strained and hollow. "I'll be back as soon as I can."

"I want to go with you!" Samantha screamed, but her dad had climbed into the front of the ambulance.

Rob touched her arm. "Sammy, let's go up to the Ivors' house and . . . drink a cup of tea," he said haltingly. "Your dad may not be back for a while."

This can't be happening. I want Mom! Samantha twisted away from Rob and ran. Her world was crashing in around her. She had to go someplace safe—but there was nowhere to go.

Blindly Samantha dashed to the barn. She skidded to a stop in the barn aisle. "Oh, no—Miracle's still running around the track!" Samantha realized. "I can't go back out there—not ever."

Suddenly Miracle put his head over his stall door and nickered. "You're here!" Samantha ran to the stall and let herself inside. In all the commotion, someone must have caught him and returned him to his stall.

Grateful for a friend, Samantha threw her arms around the horse, her tears soaking his neck. "Mom," she wept. "Mom, please come back."

Exhausted from her outburst she slid to the floor, the soft straw in the horse's stall cushioning her fall. Samantha lost all sense of time as she lay there, her heart breaking. Miracle stood over her, nosing her shoulder. The gentle black horse seemed to share her sorrow.

"Sammy?" Ian looked over the stall door.

Samantha dragged herself into a sitting position and brushed her wet hair from her face. "What?" she asked hoarsely. *Maybe he has good news!* she thought. But one look at her dad's face told her otherwise. Ian's face was drawn and haggard. He wore the saddest expression Samantha had ever seen.

"I thought I'd find you here. Come, sweetheart." Her dad held out his hand. "Let me take you home."

Samantha shook her head. She had to ask about her mother before she left the safety of the stall. She had to know if her mom was out there. But a fresh wave of terror seized Samantha, and she couldn't make herself ask that. "How's Gulfstream?" she whispered.

Ian sat in the straw beside Samantha and put his arm around her shoulders. Miracle stepped very close to them and lowered his head, as if he wanted to hear about his old trail and track companion, too. "Sammy, I'm sorry . . . but we had to put him down."

Samantha shook her head hard. How could Gulfstream, the McLeans' star horse, be gone just like that? They'd had so much hope for him! "What will Mom say?" she choked out.

Her dad pulled her close. "Oh, Sammy," he said,

rocking her as if she were a little girl again. "She won't—"

"I want Mom. Where is she?" Samantha cried.

Her dad's arms went limp, as if all the strength had suddenly gone out of them. "There's no easy way to tell you this. Samantha, your mother is dead."

5

TWO DAYS LATER SAMANTHA BENT HER HEAD, STARING AT the gaping hole in the ground. Suzanne would be buried in the small, well-tended cemetery behind the training farm.

The day was bright and pretty. The warm Florida sun spilled yellow light everywhere, and the air was crisp and clean from the rain the day before. The black clothing of the mourners looked out of place against the emerald grass and blue sky.

Mom can't be gone, Samantha thought sadly. *She can't not be seeing this lovely day. We can't be in this cemetery, saying good-bye to her like this.*

Samantha squeezed her eyes shut. Nothing about the day felt real. Her dad had told her that her mom had died instantly from a broken neck after her fall, but that was the most unreal thing of all.

For the past two days Samantha had been unable to do anything but stay in her room and cry. Her father had sat next to her on her bed, holding her hand and stroking her hair, but he'd been unable find the words to help comfort her. Samantha would never have believed she could feel so much pain. But today, all she felt was a dull, hollow ache.

"Some of us think we'll see Suzanne in heaven," the minister said. "Others will see her every day for the rest of their lives, in their memories."

If people go to heaven, I wonder where Gulfstream is? Samantha thought idly. She shook her head hard. *It doesn't matter.* She knew that Gulfstream had been humanely destroyed—he was gone forever, that was all she needed to know.

Samantha glanced around at the mourners. She had no desire to look at the gleaming brass handles and dark wood of her mother's casket.

Suzanne had been loved and admired by a lot of people, and many of them had come to the funeral. Rob Benson was there, and several other jockeys and trainers from Gulfstream, and the Ivors and Quinns. Samantha's grandparents, her mother's parents, had made the trip down from Vermont. They looked shocked and sad.

Mom would have hated this, Samantha thought suddenly as the minister closed his Bible. *She was always so happy.* Samantha squeezed her eyes shut as the casket was lowered into the ground. She was dimly aware of her father's arm around her shoulders. *I'll never be happy again*, she realized.

Ian gripped her shoulder. "It's time for us to throw a handful of dirt on the casket," he said.

Samantha shook off his hand. "I don't want to!" She couldn't stand to hear him use words like *casket*. She had refused to look at her mother during the viewing at the church.

"I'll be back soon, sweetheart," her dad said gently. The mourners parted for him to throw the first handful of dirt onto the grave.

Tiffany walked slowly toward Samantha. Samantha hadn't spoken to any of her friends since the accident. They'd all called, but she hadn't been up to talking. Now fresh tears welled up in her eyes as Tiffany hugged her close. "Oh, Sammy. If there's anything I can do to help . . ." Tiffany's usually cheerful face was streaked with tears.

Samantha just hugged her friend back. Samantha was afraid that if she tried to answer, she'd only start crying again—and never stop. *There's nothing anyone can do ever*, she thought.

The sound of loud voices carried across the cemetery. Her dad was arguing with her grandparents. Samantha suspected her grandparents had never liked her dad, but she wished they wouldn't argue today of all days. *What can they be fighting about?* she wondered unhappily. "I've got to see what's going on," she told Tiffany.

"Call me soon," Tiffany said softly.

"I will." Samantha walked slowly toward her dad and grandparents.

They didn't seem to see her. "Samantha should come live with us," said Samantha's grandmother. She was in her late sixties but still slender and energetic. Her face was flushed with anger. "You can't provide a good home for her now, Ian. Not that you ever did—"

"Don't start on that again, Sandra," Samantha's grandfather said heavily. He was older than his wife, in his seventies, with a thick mane of white hair. Today he looked even older. "But I do agree with her, Ian. Now that the child's lost her mother, she belongs in a stable environment."

Samantha stared at her grandparents in shock. *They want me to move to Vermont!* she realized. *For good. I'd never see Dad again!* It had never occurred to her that she and her dad might be separated.

Ian sighed and ran a hand through his red hair. "Well, maybe you have a point," he said slowly. "I don't really know what's ahead of me now."

For a moment Samantha tried to picture her life in Vermont. She'd be living with two old people who she barely knew, up in snow country. Her dad would never be able to get away from the racetracks to come all the way up there. And she would lose the horses! *What would I do all day long?* Samantha stifled a sob.

Samantha's grandmother turned and smiled. "There you are, honey," she said. "Come here."

Samantha stood stiffly by her grandmother. A wave of loneliness passed over her just at the thought of being left with her grandparents. *I can't lose Dad, too!* she thought. *He's all I've got.*

"Sam, dearest, we were just discussing where you'd be happiest," her grandfather began.

"I'm staying with Dad!" Samantha cried, her heart pounding.

Ian drew her close. "And I want you to stay with me—of course. But Sammy, I'm still going to be moving around from track to track. It was different when your mother was alive—she could take care of you. But I just don't know if I can provide a good life for you now."

"Yes, you can!" Samantha was so frightened, she could hardly think. "I'll take care of myself. I won't be any trouble."

Ian smiled sadly. "I know you won't. But sweetheart, I can't be happy unless I know I'm doing the right thing for you."

"I can't be happy unless I'm with you." Samantha held her breath, trying not to sob. "Mom would want us to stay together."

She threw her arms around her father, no longer trying to hold back the tears.

"Well, let's see how things go for a while if Sammy stays with you, Ian," Samantha's grandfather said sympathetically. "The child has been through a very difficult time."

Ian hesitated, looking off into the distance. "Maybe Sammy does need to be with me right now, but I do appreciate your offer. I'll keep it in mind."

Samantha let out a gasp of relief. "Thanks, Dad," she whispered.

"Honey, don't thank me." Ian hugged her fiercely. "Do you know how much I'd miss you?"

Samantha managed a tiny smile. "Me too."

I'd better be on my best behavior, she thought as she followed her father out of the cemetery. *I have to take care of myself. If I don't then Dad might change his mind and send me to Vermont. I just can't let that happen.*

"I'm going out to the barn to tie up some loose ends," Ian said the next afternoon, looking in the doorway to Samantha's room. "I'll be back soon."

Samantha jumped up. She'd been sitting in her room for hours, rearranging the makeup and brushes on her bureau. "I want to go with you," she said.

Ian frowned. It seemed to Samantha that the lines in his face had gotten deeper in the past few days. "Sammy, maybe it would be better if you didn't go out to the barn . . . at least for a while longer," he said.

"Why not?" Samantha stared at him in astonishment.

"Well, being around the barn will just bring back memories." Ian smiled sadly. "I'm not sure I want to go, either, but I have to."

"But what will I do here?" Samantha asked. She couldn't bear the thought of staying in the trailer any longer, where every empty room seemed to cry out for her mother's presence. *Mom would want me to go out to the horses*, she thought.

Ian sighed. Samantha had heard her dad pacing around the trailer all morning, as if he didn't know what to do with himself, either. "Okay, come on." He smiled a little. "I can use the company."

Samantha hurried out to the truck before he could change his mind. Ian got into the driver's side. For a moment he looked at her as if he were about to say something, but then he just started the truck.

Samantha looked out the window at the suburban streets of Miami Beach. *What should I do with the horses today?* she wondered. *Maybe just what I would do if Mom were here. I'll have to find someone to ride with, but maybe Rob or somebody is around.*

"Look, Sammy . . ." Ian cleared his throat. "There's something I want to talk to you about."

"What?" Samantha heard a serious tone in her father's voice that immediately worried her.

"When we get to the barn, I want you to be very careful." Her dad looked at her pleadingly.

"I'm always careful—you know that, Dad."

Ian sighed deeply. "Sammy, I don't want you

around the horses without supervision. And . . . I don't want you to ride."

"What?" Samantha cried. "Why?"

"Because things are different now," Ian said slowly. "Before, your mom always rode with you and took care of you. I won't have time now—"

"You don't have to take care of me!" Samantha stared at him, feeling a fresh wave of grief and loss. *Not ride again? What would Mom say?*

Don't argue, she reminded herself. *You know he doesn't mean it. He'll change his mind. He just has to.*

"Yes, I do have to take care of you," her dad was saying. He stopped the car in the parking lot at Gulfstream and looked at her. "And there's something else I need to tell you—we're leaving Miami. I just accepted a training position at Remington Park, in Oklahoma."

Samantha gasped. "I don't want to go!" she cried before she could stop herself. "That's so far away—what about my school and my friends here?" *And Mom*, she thought desperately.

"I can't stay, Sammy." Her father's voice was weary. "I just can't."

Samantha tried desperately to think of a way to change his mind. "I know you don't have"—she couldn't bring herself to say his name—"a stakes horse to train, but other owners would give you work here."

"I already promised the people at Remington." Ian

gently rested his hand on her shoulder. "We leave tomorrow. I'm sorry this is so sudden, but I think it's for the best."

The next morning Samantha threw her last suitcase into the truck. "I'm ready," she said to her dad.

"Good." Ian was packing the pieces of Samantha's bed in the storage space under the truck's camper. "Here comes the Salvation Army truck. Then we can leave."

"What are they here for?" Samantha asked. Two men climbed out of the truck, nodded to her dad, and went inside the trailer.

"To take the rest of the furniture." Ian sighed. "And your mother's things. Sammy, I know this is very hard—"

"No!" Samantha dashed into the trailer. *I thought Dad left that stuff because we were coming back some-day—not because he's giving away everything we own!*

Samantha dodged around the workers, who were carrying out the sofa, and ran into her parents' bed-room. She gasped at the sight of her mother's clothes, neatly folded on the bed.

Ian followed her into the room. "Sammy, clothes weren't the important thing about your mother," he said gently. "Somebody else can use these. That's what your mom would have wanted."

Samantha swallowed hard and looked at her feet.

A tear dropped on her shoe. "I guess so," she said. The Salvation Army workers walked into the bedroom and began gathering up her mother's familiar dresses, shoes, shirts, and jeans.

"Wait!" Samantha stopped one worker. Reaching into his pile, she pulled out a dark green, velvet dress. It had been her mother's favorite. "I'm keeping this—and her riding boots." Samantha walked over to the closet and picked up Suzanne's high black boots with the brown tops.

Ian nodded, and Samantha saw tears in his eyes. "Come on, sweetheart," he said gently. "It's time to go."

Samantha carried out the dress and boots. She climbed into the camper and carefully put the dress in her suitcase. Samantha gently stroked the dress's plush fabric. She thought she could smell her mother's perfume.

"Tiffany's here," Ian called from the cab of the truck.

Samantha shut the suitcase and backed out of the camper. Tiffany and Mrs. Rivera were getting out of their car.

"Thank you for the lovely floral arrangements," Ian said to Mrs. Rivera.

Samantha remembered the pretty flowers at the cemetery: white carnations, yellow daffodils, and yellow-and-white daisies that had spilled around the raw earth of the grave like the Florida sunshine. *Mom would have liked those,* she thought.

"You helped make them up, I bet," Samantha said to Tiffany.

Tiffany nodded slowly.

"Thank you," Samantha said, and she meant it with all her heart.

"I was glad to do it." Tiffany squeezed Samantha's hands. "Oh, Sammy. I can't believe you're really leaving."

"Neither can I," Samantha whispered.

"Sammy, we've got to hit the road." Ian rested his hand on Samantha's shoulder. "We've got a long drive ahead of us."

"Good-bye," Tiffany said softly.

"Bye." Samantha climbed into the cab of the truck and shut the door. As Ian pulled out of the driveway, she looked out the window. Tiffany was waving. Samantha waved back.

The truck turned a corner and Tiffany—and all of Samantha's old life—was suddenly gone.

"This is pretty country," Ian said early that evening.

"I guess." Samantha stretched, trying to find a comfortable position on the truck seat. They'd been driving for almost twelve hours, with only short rest stops and a quick break for lunch. She gazed out the truck window at the endless rows of cotton flashing by in Alabama. Samantha supposed the countryside was pretty to someone, but it just wasn't home to her. She sighed.

Ian glanced over at her. "You okay?" he asked.

Samantha nodded. *It's weird spending so much time with Dad,* she thought. Before, she'd always seen him at meals and at work, and he'd coached her with the horses, but they'd never spent hours and hours together. *I was always with Mom,* Samantha thought sadly.

"Look, there's a mockingbird." Ian slowed the truck and pointed out the window at a big gray-and-white bird sitting on a wire.

"Really?" Samantha stared at the bird. She'd heard the lovely, lilting songs of the mockingbird several times, but she'd never seen one before.

Samantha had to admit the drive had been kind of interesting so far. Her dad had traveled across the country so many times, he knew the names of most of the trees and birds they'd seen along the way. Samantha had enjoyed learning them.

Her dad was watching her. "Sammy, I know you're going to miss home, but I really think in some ways it's best to make a fresh start," he said. "For both of us," he added softly.

Samantha kept her head turned, looking out the window at the bird. This trip would be fun and interesting—if she could forget why they were doing it. Every time she remembered her mom, she felt fresh feelings of pain and loss so powerful, they almost overwhelmed her. Samantha was afraid of how she would feel when they got to their new house, without

70

her mom. *How can we really have a home without her?* she wondered.

But she kept quiet. *I'll have to go to Vermont if Dad thinks I'm unhappy,* she reminded herself. Samantha forced a smile. "I'll probably like Oklahoma," she said bravely.

That night Samantha tossed and turned in her sleeping bag in the truck's camper. Ian was sleeping sitting up in the cab, since there wasn't room for him to lie down in the back with all their suitcases and boxes. They'd pulled over into a rest stop after almost twenty hours of driving.

I wonder what time it is? Samantha thought, trying to see out the small window. They'd reached Oklahoma and would press on to Oklahoma City, where the Remington track was, in the morning. "It must be nearly morning now," Samantha murmured.

She flopped onto her stomach, trying to get comfortable on the crowded truck bed. Suitcases were piled around her head, and the desk lamps and uneven piles of clothes formed strange shadows under the orange light of the rest stop.

Something hit her on the head. Samantha groaned, then groped in the dark for the object. "Oh, it's you," she said softly. It was one of her mom's riding boots.

Samantha hugged the boot tight. Slowly she felt herself drifting off to sleep.

She was riding Miracle on the familiar trails at Ivor Stables with her mother. Samantha was surprised to see her mother on Gulfstream—hadn't something happened to him? But she was relieved he was okay after all. "I've signed up for the last courses I need to finish my college degree, Samantha," Suzanne said. "I'll be so happy when I graduate."

Samantha smiled broadly. She was glad that her mom would be finishing college. She has plans, *Samantha thought.* She's not dead—that was just a big mistake.

Suddenly Gulfstream was galloping out of control, heading straight for the rail. Samantha realized she had to stop him—but with a sickening sense of fear, she knew she couldn't. She'd been dreaming before, but this was reality. Her mother was going to die.

"Mom!" Samantha sat bolt upright, hitting her head on the camper's low ceiling. She gripped her mother's riding boot in terror, digging her fingers into the soft, well-worn leather. Her body shuddering with sobs, Samantha dropped back onto the pillow and cuddled her mother's boot in her arms. "At least I have you," she whispered. "You're all I have left of her."

6

"SAMMY, WAKE UP, SWEETIE." IAN WAS SHAKING HER FOOT.

"Where are we?" Samantha yawned, sitting up as straight as she could in the camper. Light was just beginning to seep through the windows.

"Oklahoma, remember?"

"Oh, yeah." Samantha crawled to the edge of the truck's open tailgate and looked out. The huge Oklahoma sky, a dome of robin's-egg blue, rested on top of flat, tan land. It was so early, only truckers were rolling out of the rest stop. Their gears roared as they merged back onto the interstate.

"We're almost to our new house," Ian said. "Let's grab some breakfast, then drive out there."

"Okay," Samantha said. She wanted to get to the house quickly, too. *I can't wait to get out of the truck,* she thought. *In our house we can eat real food and sleep on real beds.*

"Where is the house?" she asked as she got in the cab with her dad.

"Near Oklahoma City. Out in the country," Ian replied, starting the truck.

"Oh." *That sounds neat*, Samantha thought. She remembered how pretty the Florida countryside was. She'd always wished they could move out of the trailer park.

Across the Oklahoma landscape dozens of oil derricks slowly, determinedly bobbed up and down as they searched for oil. Most of the countryside was fields, with young spring crops pushing up through the soil.

Ian turned the truck onto a dirt road lined with flat green fields. Samantha could see a few small ranch houses scattered in the distance. A few minutes later Ian pulled into a driveway. "This is it," he said.

Samantha saw a small house perched on the edge of a field. A couple of spindly oaks out front bent in the strong wind. *That house is as small as our trailer was!* she thought in disappointment. Squeezing her eyes shut, Samantha tried not to think about the beautiful farm her parents had planned to buy.

Ian was carrying their suitcases into the house. "Come on inside, Sammy," he called over his shoulder. "Let's get settled."

Samantha straightened her shoulders and followed him. *Okay, don't whine*, she ordered herself. *Try to act like Mom would.*

"Here's your bedroom." Ian pointed to an empty, white-painted room. "It's nearest to the bathroom."

Samantha walked over to the window and looked out. The window took up most of the wall—it was almost like being outside in the big field. *That's nice, I guess*, she thought. Florida was flat and open, too.

"Is your room okay? I had to rent this place sight unseen." Her dad was standing in the doorway, a concerned expression on his face. "I know you like the country," he added. "So I told the real estate agent to find us something out of the city."

Samantha managed a smile. "Thanks, Dad. I'll bring in some more of our things."

She pulled the nearest box out of the back of the truck and carried it into the living room. It was almost too heavy for her, and she dropped it with a thump. The box popped open, spilling a couple of forks on the floor. Her mom had bought that heavy, beautiful silverware at a flea market. It looked so forlorn on the bare floor. *I don't know how I'm going to make this place home, but I have to try*, she thought.

For the next hour Samantha put away their belongings and moved the furniture around. Finally she'd arranged what they had to her satisfaction. It didn't take long: The house only had five rooms—two bedrooms, a kitchen, a living room, and the bathroom.

"Great job, Sammy," her dad said approvingly, glancing around the living room. "Thanks, honey."

"This still isn't right." Samantha frowned at the chairs she'd set near the window so they could see the view. "The house is so empty," she said, and immediately regretted her words.

Ian looked at her sadly. "Maybe we need to buy some more furniture," he suggested. "Oh, Sammy. I'm so sorry . . . about everything. We'll do whatever you want." Ian held open his arms.

Samantha ran to him and hugged him. "So let's buy some more furniture," she said, her voice muffled against his shoulder. *Mom would,* Samantha told herself. *She wouldn't live in an empty house.*

Ian stroked her hair. "Do you want to go to the track with me?" he asked. "I have to look over the horses I'll be training."

"Sure." Samantha smiled up at him with genuine enthusiasm. She'd been to many race tracks around the country, but never to Remington.

"Let's go." Ian opened the front door. Samantha noticed he didn't lock it after them. She supposed there wasn't any reason to out here.

A few minutes later Ian turned the truck in to a giant parking lot. "Here's the track," he said.

"Wow, this place is new!" Samantha said in surprise. She realized she'd expected the Remington track to be second-rate after Gulfstream. Samantha jumped out of the truck and hurried to keep up with her long-legged father as he strode toward the entrance to the track.

Samantha walked across the polished, airy lobby and looked out the glass doors to the track. "Nice," she said approvingly. The cloudless blue sky made the track look bigger. A swath of trees surrounded it, their leaves the soft, spearmint color of spring.

Ian smiled. "I'm glad you like it. Let's go meet the horses," he said.

As Samantha and her dad walked toward the barns Ian nodded and said hello to a few people who looked like trainers or grooms. He stepped inside one of the barns and pointed. "My horses are these six right here."

Five of the horses were looking over their stall doors. Three were chestnuts, one was a red roan, and the other was a flea-bitten gray. Samantha couldn't help smiling at the horses' hopeful expressions. "Hi, guys," she said softly.

"I'm going to check some charts in the office," Ian said. "What do you want to do?"

"Get to know the horses, of course." Samantha stepped closer to the stalls.

The gray tossed his head and pinned his ears. "Sammy, please don't go near them!" Ian warned. The fear in his voice was plain.

"I'll watch out until they get to know me," Samantha said, unable to keep the impatience out of her voice. *I've only been around horses my whole life,* she added to herself.

Ian rubbed his forehead. "Sammy, I have to go to my meeting. I can't stay here and watch you."

Samantha groaned. She'd hoped her dad had forgotten what he'd said about her being around the horses, but apparently he hadn't. He seemed stricter than ever. "I won't go near the horses," she finally said. "I'll just look at them."

"Good." Her dad sounded very relieved. "I'll just be a minute."

"Okay." Samantha could tell that arguing with him wouldn't do any good now.

She walked down the row of horses, staying out of their reach. Samantha couldn't tell much about their conformation since they were in stalls, but from their heads she thought they looked like nice enough horses. None of them had run in stakes races, though.

Samantha reached the end of the row. The last horse still hadn't shown its head. "Where are you?" she murmured, venturing closer. Samantha saw the horse moving around in the shadows at the back of its stall. It looked chestnut or brown—in the dim light Samantha couldn't see if the mare had the red highlights of a chestnut. "Come here, pretty girl," she said quietly. "I just want to get a look at you."

The horse stopped moving. A moment later she stepped to the stall door.

"That's it," Samantha soothed, lifting her hand to rub the mare's nose. "So you are a chestnut."

"Sammy, no!" Ian cried. Her dad ran down the aisle and grabbed her arm. "What are you thinking!" The mare jumped to the back of her stall in fright.

"Sorry," Samantha said. Her heart was hammering from the shock of her dad's loud voice and the horse's sudden movement.

Ian sighed and put a hand on her shoulder. "I'm sorry I yelled at you. I was just so worried."

"That's okay." Samantha's heart was still racing. She drew a deep breath. "So what's the story with this horse—why is she so shy?"

"Satin Doll spent most of her career in the claiming cellar," Ian said. "Now she's injured her ankle, and I think it still hurts her. I'm going to try to bring her back up to the best form I can, but I'm not expecting much."

With her dad beside her, Samantha stepped closer to the stall. Satin Doll stood huddled at the very back. She was small for a Thoroughbred, not much more than fifteen hands tall, and had a narrow blaze and star. She still hadn't shed out her raggedy winter coat and she looked shaggy and neglected. Satin Doll gazed at Samantha with a timid expression in her big brown eyes.

You poor thing, Samantha thought, her heart going out to the unhappy horse. "Dad, can I groom her?" she asked. "She seems really gentle. And you can see she really needs a good brushing."

Her father looked conflicted. "No, I don't think

so," he finally said. "Even a horse as nice as this one is capable of kicking or striking if she were startled."

Samantha tried to hide her disappointment. *Dad's being totally unreasonable,* she thought. *But what can I do?*

"Come on, Sammy," Ian said. He walked back and put his arm around her shoulders. "Let's go look at furniture."

"Okay." Samantha reluctantly left the stall. At the sound of a soft nicker she looked back.

Satin Doll was gazing sadly over her stall door. She seemed to be saying she wanted Samantha to stay but didn't have much hope that she would.

Samantha walked back to the stall and stood a safe distance away. The mare timidly stretched her neck toward Samantha, as if she wished they could be friends. "Sorry, girl," Samantha whispered. "Tell you what—I'll bring you some carrots the next time I come."

The mare whickered throatily and bobbed her head.

I wonder if she's ever had a carrot, Samantha thought as she rejoined her father. *I just wish Dad would change his mind about letting me groom her. Besides, if I don't help with the horses, I won't have anything to do but school. And I don't know if that's going to work out, either.*

*   *   *

Samantha walked uncertainly down the hall in her new junior high school, wondering if she was going in the right direction for her sixth-period English class. Ian had registered her at the front office, then left with a reassuring smile.

But Samantha felt far from reassured. "This school is so small," she murmured. "Everybody's going to notice I'm the new kid." She remembered how comfortable she'd been at her big, old school in Miami. She'd known lots of people, and she'd had Tiffany to hang out with.

"Room four," Samantha said. "Okay, that's it." She stood outside the classroom door, trying to get up the nerve to go in. "Just do it," she ordered herself finally. "Stop thinking!"

Samantha grabbed the doorknob and opened the door so hard, it slammed back into the wall. All the kids looked up from their books and stared.

"You must be Samantha McLean." The teacher smiled warmly at her. "Come in," she said. "I'm Mrs. Kendall." She pointed to a seat by the window. "There's a free desk right over there."

Samantha stumbled toward the desk, glad she would be sitting down. She saw a blond girl laugh, then bend over to say something to the girl next to her.

I hope she's not be laughing at me! Samantha sat quickly at the desk and arranged her books. She hoped everyone would forget about her.

"Samantha, why don't you tell us a little about yourself before we get back to the lesson?" Mrs. Kendall asked.

Samantha could feel a flush creeping over her face. She had trouble talking in front of people. "Well . . ." She cleared her throat. "I'm Samantha McLean, and my dad trained horses at Gulfstream Park near Miami. We . . . had a stakes horse there who won the Donn. My dad's training at Remington now."

To Samantha's horror, she heard a ripple of laughter run through the classroom. *What?* she thought frantically. Then she saw that a gangly, red-haired boy in the back had his hand on his hip and was tossing his head. He was imitating her!

How dare he? Samantha thought indignantly. Glaring at the boy and the whole class, she sat back down. Mrs. Kendall resumed the English lesson.

"Hey . . . um . . . Samantha," whispered the blond girl behind her.

"What?" Samantha half turned in her seat, still flipping pages in her English textbook. She couldn't figure out where the teacher was.

"What do you call those weird things you're wearing?" the girl whispered.

"Clothes," Samantha snapped, but she could feel her face heating up again. She'd noticed that the kids here dressed up a lot more than the kids at her old school. The blond girl wore a beige corduroy jumper with a black turtleneck. Samantha felt totally out of place in her jeans and T-shirt.

The girl's friend giggled. "I call those ranch hand clothes."

"Kelly, Lynne—," Mrs. Kendall called. "Quiet, please."

The two girls didn't say anything more, but Samantha could hear muffled giggles. *I don't care*, she thought, but her heart ached with loneliness.

For the rest of the day a few kids glanced at her, but nobody spoke. *They must think I don't know how to dress*, Samantha thought miserably, remembering how she and her mom would pick out just the right outfit for her first day of school each year.

After school Samantha sprinted gladly to her dad's truck. *I'm ready to get out of here*, she thought. *Maybe I can go out to see the horses. Horses are a lot easier to understand than people!*

"Hi, sweetheart," Ian said as she opened the door. "How was your day? Did you make any friends?"

"A few." Samantha slammed the door. Pride wouldn't let her admit to her dad how the day had really gone.

"That's good." Ian drummed his fingers on the steering wheel. "I've got to run back to the barn and work on my books, but I'll bring something home for dinner. I'll take you to the house so you can get started on your homework."

Samantha felt a quick rush of disappointment.

She'd counted on seeing Satin Doll again. "I want to go out to the barn with you," she said.

"No, you should do your homework." Ian reached over to pat her hand. "I really won't be long."

Samantha bit her lip. She wondered how she would stand being alone after a day like she'd had. She and her dad had bought a new couch and a few other pieces of furniture, but it hadn't been delivered yet. The house would still be echoing and strange.

The moment Ian dropped her off at the house, Samantha ran to the portable phone and punched in Tiffany's number. "Please be there," she said to herself. Tiffany had cheerleading practice and a lot of other after-school activities.

"Hello?" Tiffany said.

"You are home!" Samantha flopped down onto her desk chair and sighed with relief. It was great to hear her friend's upbeat voice.

"I'm so glad you called!" Tiffany said excitedly.

"I needed to hear a friendly voice." Samantha kicked off her shoes. "The kids at my new school are real jerks. I think they all hate me."

"Sammy, they'll like you once they get to know you," Tiffany stated positively.

"Somehow I doubt it," Samantha said glumly.

"So what's Oklahoma like?" Tiffany wanted to know.

"Oh, kind of pretty. We live in the country."

Samantha looked around her mostly empty room. "The track's nice," she added.

"Well, that's important. Look, Sammy, try not to be depressed. I bet you'll meet somebody fun."

"I guess." Samantha frowned. "So how's everybody at school?" she asked.

Tiffany giggled. "Do you mean Jason? He's fine. And guess what? Nick asked me out to a movie next weekend!"

"Wow, Tiffany! That's so great!" Samantha said softly.

"Yeah." Tiffany sighed. "Oh, Sammy, I miss you—things just aren't the same without you. I don't have anyone to talk to."

"I'll be back someday," Samantha said quickly. *Somehow I'll get back to Miami—and to Tiffany and Mom.*

"I hope so." Tiffany's voice was low. "I mean, that's what I tell myself—we were such good friends, you can't be gone for good."

"Let me give you my phone number," Samantha said. "Then you can call if anything important happens."

"I'll call you really soon," Tiffany promised.

Samantha gave Tiffany her phone number and said good-bye. She swallowed hard as she stared at the silent phone. Tiffany was so far away. "I can't call her every night," she murmured.

Not knowing what else to do, Samantha sat at

her desk and opened her English book. The jeers of the other kids in her class rang in her ears. *I don't care about them,* she said to herself. *I'll just think about Mom when they make fun of me. She thought I was beautiful.*

She bent her head closer to the book and swallowed hard, fighting back her tears.

7

THE NEXT MORNING BEFORE SCHOOL, SAMANTHA DROVE
out to the track again with her dad. "Remember,
Sammy," Ian said as they ordered breakfast at a
drive-through restaurant. "When we get to the track,
don't—"

"I know." Samantha stifled a groan. "Don't go anywhere near the horses."

"Sammy, believe me, it's for your own good," her
dad said earnestly.

Then why don't I feel good about it? Samantha
thought in frustration as her dad handed her the takeout bag with their breakfast in it.

"I know it's going to be hard for you to stay away
from the horses," her dad said as they drove toward
the track. "I might have time to supervise you in a
couple of weeks. But Sammy, sweetie, if you're not

having fun, you can go stay with your grandparents. You know they'd love to have you—"

"I'm having fun," Samantha said quickly. A sick feeling of fear rose in her stomach, and she set her English muffin on top of the bag, her appetite gone. *I'd better watch my step,* she thought.

In the barn at Remington, Samantha followed her dad down the aisle, careful to stay out of reach of inquisitive noses. She had to smile when Satin Doll popped her head out of her stall and looked out expectantly as Samantha and her dad approached.

Samantha noticed that the mare hadn't been groomed. Samantha's fingers itched to get out brushes and clippers. "Dad, can't I please groom Satin Doll?" she asked. "I mean, look at her!"

"No." Ian turned away. "Even grooming horses is too dangerous."

"What am I supposed to do?" Samantha demanded, frustrated. "Muck out stalls?"

"I guess you can do that. I'll see you in about an hour—I've got a meeting with a couple of owners." Ian walked down the aisle, looking distracted.

Samantha threw up her hands. "Oh, great, cleaning stalls," she muttered. "But it's better than nothing, I suppose."

She quickly gathered a pitchfork, shovel, and wheelbarrow out of the storage shed at the end of the barn. "I'd better get started before Dad remembers I'll have to touch the horses even to clean the stalls,"

Samantha murmured. She'd have to put them in crossties to get them out of her way.

Samantha wheeled the tools to Satin Doll's stall. "Let's start with you," she said. "I think you'll be the easiest."

Satin Doll suddenly lunged at the stall door, as if she'd figured out that Samantha was about to open it.

Startled, Samantha shrank back. She hadn't been around horses—hadn't even patted one—since the terrible day of her mother's accident. *Am I afraid of them?* she wondered. *How can that be? I love horses more than anything in the world!*

Samantha lifted her hand to open the stall door but dropped it swiftly. "Can I really do this?" she wondered aloud. "The last horse I worked with was Miracle—and look what I did! If I'd done the right thing that day, Mom would be alive now." Samantha chewed her trembling lip, trying to decide what to do. *And what if Dad sees this?* she thought. *He won't like it, even though he did tell me I could clean stalls.*

Satin Doll had stopped moving, as if she sensed Samantha's indecision. She stood quietly, her dark eyes fixed imploringly on Samantha.

"Oh, you poor girl." Samantha's heart melted. "I can't leave you in there like that. Taking care of you has to be the right thing to do. I know Mom would want me to."

Samantha looked swiftly around. No one was in sight, and her dad had said he'd be meeting with several owners—that should take him at least an hour. She'd just have to hope none of them wanted to come look at their horses.

Satin Doll was bobbing her head and pushing against the door with her chest. "I'll bet you haven't been out in days," Samantha said, grabbing a lead rope from a hook next to the stall. "Sorry, girl, but we're not going far."

Samantha opened the stall door and automatically moved to intercept the eager horse as she pushed out the door. Samantha's hands were quick and accurate from years of experience. *I can do this*, she thought, feeling a quick rush of pleasure. She expertly clipped Satin Doll in crossties.

Humming to herself, Samantha pushed the wheelbarrow into the stall and mucked it out. She enjoyed the familiar routine and was even grateful for the pangs in her muscles as they adjusted to the familiar exercise.

"Okay, you're done," Samantha said after she had spread around a thick layer of fresh straw. Now Satin Doll had a clean, comfortable stall. Samantha nodded with satisfaction.

Satin Doll turned as far as she could in the crossties to look at her. Samantha noticed again the mare's heavy, matted coat and the bits of straw stuck to it. "Seems like a shame to put such a dirty horse in such a clean stall," she said. "I bet you don't like looking like that—I wouldn't."

Samantha came to a quick decision. She unclipped the mare and put her in her stall, where she would be less visible. Looking around nervously, Samantha opened the mare's trunk and selected currycomb, dandy, and body brushes. "I'm going to brush you," she said firmly. "Somebody's got to do it." Samantha's stomach felt a little queasy, but she felt happier than she had in recent memory.

This time Samantha entered the stall without hesitation. Satin Doll looked at her uneasily, ears pricked, but she stood still.

"You're not too sure about people, are you?" Samantha asked gently. "Don't worry—I think you'll like this."

The mare quivered as Samantha carefully ran the metal currycomb over her neck. "Easy, girl," she soothed. "This is a new experience, huh? Nobody's had a brush on you in a long time, I bet."

I'm not afraid of her anymore, Samantha realized. She hugged the mare's neck. "I'll come here every day and make you look beautiful," she promised. "Just like Mom did for me." Samantha brushed away a tear that trickled slowly down her cheek.

"I can't believe the difference in this mare," Ian said one morning a few weeks later. One of the older grooms, Vinny Talbert, was holding Satin Doll outside the barn while Ian looked her over.

Samantha smiled. Satin Doll's chestnut coat gleamed softly under the overcast sky, and her alert eyes moved quickly from Ian to Vinny to Samantha. She bobbed her head at Samantha, arching her neck, and nickered.

Vinny winked at Samantha. "Hey, she seems to like you," he said.

"That's funny." Samantha looked at her feet, hoping Vinny would be quiet. The older groom had caught her several times in Satin Doll's stall, brushing the mare. Vinny wasn't the only track worker who knew about Samantha's work. Samantha's care of Satin Doll was an open secret on the backside.

Thank goodness nobody told Dad, she thought gratefully. Samantha knew she was risking her life by grooming the mare—but not in the way her dad thought. *If he knew how much I've been around Satin Doll, he'd send me to my grandparents in a heartbeat,* she thought, wiping her sweaty palms on her jeans.

"Satin Doll's clockings have been excellent—her injury seems to have completely cleared up," Ian went on. "I've entered her in a ten-thousand-dollar claiming race in a couple of weeks."

"Super!" Samantha said excitedly. Her dad looked pleased, too—for the first time since Suzanne's death.

Grooming Satin was worth the risk, Samantha thought, looking fondly at the pretty mare. *Besides, the people at the track are so nice to me. I don't think Dad's ever going to find out.*

"Well, let's go," Ian said. "Time for school, Samantha."

Samantha stifled a groan. Tiffany had been wrong when she said that the situation at school would get better. If anything, the kids were meaner.

"Yuck!" Kelly exclaimed as Samantha walked into their science classroom a few minutes later.

Samantha stared at the other girl. *I really don't know what your problem is,* she thought, turning her back on Kelly. *I just wish it wasn't my problem.*

Mr. Foyle, the science teacher, looked up from his desk and frowned. "Is something wrong, Kelly?"

"No." Kelly smiled innocently at the teacher. Mr. Foyle smiled back.

Samantha chewed on a fingernail, trying to control her temper. *Kelly's the reason no one likes me at this school,* she thought. Kelly was the most popular girl at the small school—everybody listened to what she had to say.

"Pick lab partners," Mr. Foyle said to the class.

Oh, no, not again. Samantha groaned silently. *No one's going to want to be my partner.*

She sat alone at her desk, staring at her hands, while the other kids picked partners and moved to the lab stations at the back of the room. Nobody so much as looked in her direction.

Mr. Foyle got up from his desk. "Samantha still doesn't have a partner and neither do you, Kelly. Why don't you girls work together?"

"Mr. Foyle, I only don't have a partner because Lynne's sick," Kelly said quickly. "I can work by myself today."

"Work with Samantha," Mr. Foyle said impatiently. "Why not?"

Kelly rolled her eyes. "Oh, okay," she said.

"What is the matter with you?" Samantha snapped as she followed Kelly back to a lab station.

Kelly opened a drawer and began taking out beakers, test tubes, and corks. "You could help me with the experiment," she said.

Samantha put her hands on her hips. "Not until you tell me what's wrong with everybody here."

"What's wrong with *us*?" Kelly snorted and rummaged in the drawer. "I just don't want to work with Miss Supersnob from Gulfstream."

"It's not that I'm a snob . . ." Samantha stopped. Maybe Kelly had a point. Maybe she was always comparing her life here to her life in Miami. "I just miss home," she said finally. "I think the track here is really nice."

"You should," Kelly said, her tone softening a little. "My dad works out there in the racing office."

"Oh. I didn't know that." *What a dork I've been,* Samantha said to herself.

Silently Samantha began to worm a piece of glass

94

tubing through a cork for their experiment. She wondered if she should apologize to Kelly.

Kelly filled a beaker with water and set it down on the counter. She gave Samantha a long, searching look. As if she'd finally made some decision, she smiled. "Do you want to eat lunch with me today?" she asked. "I can tell you stuff about Remington—if you want to know."

"I do want to know! I mean, sure," Samantha said quickly.

"We can talk horses." Kelly looked at their chemistry textbook to see what they had to do next.

Samantha nodded, relief washing over her. Finally she wouldn't have to sit alone at one of the long cafeteria tables. *Maybe I've finally made a friend,* she thought.

"Satin Doll looks beautiful," Kelly said admiringly three weeks later in the saddling paddock at Remington.

Samantha just nodded, unable to speak around the lump in her throat. She handed her dad the mare's small racing saddle. In a few minutes Satin Doll would run in her first race since her injury, a claiming race at seven furlongs.

Satin Doll stamped an impatient hoof as Ian tightened the girth. "You really want to get out there, don't you?" Samantha asked.

The mare bobbed her head as if to say, "Of

course!" The dull expression was gone from her eyes, and her russet coat sparkled in the sunlight.

Samantha sighed as she stared at the mare. Satin Doll obviously looked and felt wonderful. The only problem was, after the race Ian wouldn't be training her anymore. The mare's good looks hadn't gone unnoticed, and a new owner had claimed her. After the race she would go home with him.

"I'll take her around the walking ring," Ian said as he critically examined Satin Doll's tack.

"Come on—let's go wait with Carl Howell, Satin's jockey," Samantha said to Kelly.

"Sure. This is fun!" Kelly grinned.

"I guess." Samantha tried to feel upbeat, but she just couldn't. Satin Doll was her horse in every way that counted, but she was going to lose her.

A few minutes later Ian led the mare over to Carl Howell. The jockey looked her over carefully, then sprang into the saddle with a hand from Ian. "She looks a lot better than she did last summer," Carl said. He sounded surprised.

"She does seem like a different horse these days," Ian agreed.

Satin Doll stepped closer to Samantha, sniffing her front pockets for carrots. *Uh-oh,* Samantha thought, trying to push the mare's nose away. *Don't blow our cover.*

"Samantha, stay back!" Ian grabbed her arm and pulled her out of Satin Doll's reach. The mare gave a surprised snort and half reared.

"Dad, stop it—you're scaring her!" Samantha angrily shrugged off his hand.

"She seems to know you pretty well," Kelly whispered.

"Yeah," Samantha said quietly. Much as she liked Kelly now, she hadn't told her about Satin Doll. Then she'd have to explain why she had to groom the mare in secret—and Samantha couldn't bring herself to talk about her mom with anyone.

"Take Satin Doll straight to the lead," Ian instructed Carl. "Don't let her get shuffled to the back of the pack. She's gotten discouraged when that happened in her other races and she's fallen off the pace."

Carl shrugged. "Okay. We'll see how she does."

Carl turned Satin Doll toward the track. Samantha glanced to see if her dad was watching, but he was looking at a horse in the walking ring. Samantha patted the mare on the flank. "Run your best, sweetie," she said.

Satin Doll looked around and nickered. Then she marched off purposefully, following the rest of the field.

"I bet Satin Doll wins it," Kelly said as she, Samantha, and Ian walked to the stands.

"Me, too." Samantha wondered what would happen if the mare ran badly. Maybe she would drop down in the claiming ranks again, and Ian would get to retrain her. *But I can't hope for that*, she scolded herself.

"The horses are in the gate," the announcer called a few minutes later. "And they're off!"

Satin Doll plunged out of the gate, fighting for position among the ten horses in the field. Samantha's heart sank as the mare dropped back behind the front-runners.

"She broke badly!" Samantha cried.

"The other horses just broke better," Ian said philosophically, training his binoculars on the field.

Samantha watched in dismay as Satin Doll fell from fifth place to eighth as the horses galloped around the turn. This race was so short, only seven furlongs. Satin Doll looked completely out of contention!

"Don't give up on her, Carl," Ian said, as if he were reading Samantha's mind.

"He's got to trust her!" Samantha scanned the field frantically with her own binoculars. Satin Doll had picked off a few of the fading front-runners, but four horses still pounded down the track ahead of her. Kelly squeezed Samantha's knee sympathetically.

"I don't know if she's got the heart to fight back." Ian shook his head.

"Yes, she does!" Samantha said fiercely.

"You don't know that."

Samantha bit her lip. *I do, too!*

Satin Doll swung into the stretch, her strides long and fluid. Samantha could feel her hopes rising. The mare was running so well—she didn't look like she was tiring at all. *Come on*, Samantha silently urged. *Come on* . . .

"And it's Satin Doll, coming under a ride now," the announcer said. "She's making her move on the inside!"

Samantha wrung her hands as Satin Doll passed Puff of Smoke, the black colt in fourth, and Yank's Fife, a chestnut in third. "She's putting them away!" Samantha cried. "Go, girl! Just two more and you've got it!"

"The track's been favoring the rail all day," Ian said. "Maybe she does have a shot at it!"

"Satin Doll strikes out for the lead," the announcer called.

For a moment Samantha had no idea if Satin Doll could do it. The mare had to find more—but the wire was just ahead!

Satin Doll whipped by the second-place horse on the inside. But Splendid Bid, the last horse ahead of her, was still running strongly.

"Please, Satin," Samantha whispered. "Give it everything you've got—don't be afraid. You know you want to win!"

The mare seemed to hear. With one final bound she shot up to Splendid Bid. They were neck and neck . . . Satin Doll put her nose under the wire first!

"She's won it," Ian said in disbelief.

"Yes!" Samantha turned to Kelly, and the two girls grinned at each other.

"I have to admit I'm surprised," Ian said. "I thought she'd make a good show, but I didn't think she'd win the first time out. Her new owner should be very pleased."

At her dad's words Samantha felt her excitement drain out of her.

"Let's get down to the winner's circle," Ian said. "The former owner isn't here—he hasn't seen Satin Doll in weeks. He didn't think it would be worth his while to see her run."

"Well, he was wrong." Samantha swallowed her tears. As proud as she was for Satin Doll, she hated the thought of losing her.

Carl was waiting at the winner's circle with Satin Doll. The mare was prancing proudly and chewing at the bit. *You look like a racehorse again,* Samantha thought. *I did the right thing by helping you. I'm sure of it now.*

"Pretty horse," said a photographer, snapping a picture.

"Yes, she'll be one to watch," responded a reporter.

Samantha tried not to cry as her dad moved her to the left in the winner's circle—away from Satin Doll. *Don't you dare cry in front of all these people!* she ordered herself fiercely.

"Okay, we're done here. That's her new trainer." Ian pointed to a middle-aged man standing on the other side of the winner's circle. "He'll take the horse."

Satin Doll looked at Samantha and nickered softly, the way she had the very first day Samantha saw her. "Good-bye, girl," Samantha whispered. Kelly gazed at her sympathetically, but Samantha knew she couldn't understand. Samantha turned away to hide her tears.

If only I could really say good-bye to her, she thought. *But then Dad would know what I've done.* Samantha's eyes burned. The lovely mare walked off behind her new trainer, her strides long and confident. They vanished behind the crowd, out of Samantha's life.

I might as well face it—I'm going to lose everything I love sooner or later, she thought sadly.

8

SEVERAL WEEKS LATER SAMANTHA EXAMINED THE MENU closely at the fast-food restaurant where she and her father had eaten breakfast every day in the two months they'd been at Remington. *I think I've ordered everything on the menu about twelve times,* she decided. *Unless I want a hot fudge sundae for breakfast.*

Samantha frowned. She knew her dad would take her someplace nicer to eat if she asked—he just didn't think about those things. Sometimes Samantha longed for a home-cooked meal. But she didn't want to complain.

"Scrambled eggs and a toasted English muffin," Samantha told the person behind the counter.

"Let's eat here this morning," Ian said from behind her.

"Don't you want to get out to the horses?"

102

Samantha asked, surprised. She and her dad always ordered takeout at the restaurant, then ate on the way to the track.

Samantha was anxious to get to the barn. Satin Doll was gone, but Samantha had a new secret project—gentling Sometimes Blue, the gray gelding her dad trained who was so nasty to people. So far, she'd gotten him to let her walk up to him without laying back his ears. Some mornings Samantha thought he even looked glad to see her. Part of the problem, she knew, was that the exercise rider smacked Sometimes Blue for his bad behavior. The gelding just acted worse then.

That's not what I'd do if I rode him, Samantha thought as she took a seat across from her dad.

Ian stirred his coffee and looked across the table at Samantha. "How would you feel about another move, Sammy?" he asked.

Samantha stared at him, shocked. "Why? The meet isn't over!"

"I've been offered a job at Hollywood Park." Her dad frowned thoughtfully. "The horses I'll be training are better than the ones here."

"Well, um . . . Hollywood Park's a fantastic track." Samantha's thoughts were whirling. She really didn't want to leave Remington anymore, no matter how great the horses and track were at Hollywood Park. *Why do we have to leave just when I've found some friends and settled in here?* she thought.

Her dad reached across the table and took her hand. "I'm glad you don't mind," he said. "We'll have to leave in a week. Now that you're not around the horses so much, it might be fun for you to be in a city like Los Angeles. I know it's been hard for you—not being able to spend a lot of time with the horses."

Samantha just nodded. She remembered how hard it had been for her to adjust to the move here. *I don't want to do that again so soon,* she thought. *But how can I tell Dad?*

She became aware of her dad's intense stare and quickly forced a smile. But he must have seen that she was depressed. "Maybe this isn't the right thing for you." He sighed. "Maybe you *should* try staying with your grandparents. Your life would have more of a routine."

"No!" Samantha said quickly. "It's exciting—all the change." Her heart was thudding with fright. "California's fine with me."

A week later Samantha hurried through the bustling Los Angeles airport with her dad, trying not to lose him in the crowd. Luckily his red hair made him easy to spot. "Where are we going first?" she asked breathlessly.

"Let's go straight to the track." Ian stepped through the glass doors of the terminal and hailed a taxi.

Samantha tossed her suitcase in the trunk. She felt a pang as she looked at her small dark blue canvas bag. It held all the possessions she had left in the world. Anything that couldn't go on the plane had to be left in Oklahoma.

It was just stuff, Samantha tried to console herself. But she couldn't help remembering that she'd had to give up her very favorite piece of furniture, the antique bed that her mom had bought for her.

She drew a deep breath. *At least I'm here with Dad,* she reminded herself. *I'm going to be around horses.*

As the taxi drove to the track Samantha looked out the window at the new city. With its palm trees and wide streets, Los Angeles looked something like Miami. *Maybe this will be okay,* she hoped.

The taxi dropped them off in the parking lot at the track. In the distance Samantha could hear the announcer calling a race.

"Can I watch a race?" Samantha asked.

"I guess so." Ian looked at her for a moment. "Do you think you can find me on the backside afterward? I have to talk to another trainer for about an hour."

"Sure," Samantha said. *Dad's forgotten I can even find my way around a track,* she thought with frustration. *He'll never give me any responsibility with the horses!*

"I'll introduce you to my new horses when I get

back." Ian smiled. "I think you'll like them—they're top-quality allowance horses."

"Okay." *Maybe Dad will let me help with them,* she hoped.

Samantha bought a program in the clubhouse, then walked out to the track. Since it was a weekday, there weren't many spectators. Several older men had been in the clubhouse, sitting comfortably at little tables in front of TVs simulcasting races from other tracks.

"I don't know why anybody would want to be inside on a day like this," Samantha murmured. The sun, now high in the sky, was bright and soothing on her face. Closing her eyes, Samantha could imagine she was back at Gulfstream. *Mom will come join me in a minute,* she thought. *We'll spend a day at the races together.*

Her eyes flew open at the sound of a loud snort. The horses for the next race were emerging from the tunnel for the post parade.

Samantha felt a flash of searing disappointment. For a second, her dream had seemed so real. "I'll just act like I would if Mom were here," she decided.

Samantha watched closely as the first horse, a glossy dapple gray, marched by her with his jockey up. The horse's strides were free-swinging, and his slender legs were unblemished by any swelling or scars. "Nice," Samantha breathed.

The gray was followed by a dazzling black colt, his

106

eyes so dark they melted into the color of his smooth coat. All the horses in the field held their heads high, and their gaze was proud.

"Satin Doll was beautiful, but she wasn't in the same league as you gorgeous guys," Samantha murmured. "So, who do I like to win?" she asked herself, looking at her program. Samantha leaned over the fence to see the horses better until a track guard frowned at her. They were all superb animals, but she decided to go with the dapple gray. According to her program, his name was Prospector's Whimsy.

The nine-horse field loaded quickly into the gate. Then total silence charged with expectation fell over the track.

The sound of the starting bell cut through the humid air and the horses broke from the gate, a jumble of struggling bodies as the jockeys fought for position. Bunched together tightly, the horses roared by the stands for the first time.

"And Prospector's Whimsy takes a short lead," the announcer said. "Tropical Delight looms just behind him. Magenta Mile is in third. . . ."

The horses pounded by the wire for the first time, throwing clods of the soft track high in the air. Samantha knew she should back up to get out of the way, but she felt mesmerized by the power, grace, and speed of the top Thoroughbreds. A fine spray of sand dusted her face as the horses shot into the first turn.

"Prospector's Whimsy is beginning to pick up the pace at the half-mile pole," the announcer said. "Back one, no, two to Tropical Delight. Snowy Gulch is running in third, with Magenta Mile sitting off the pace in fourth."

Samantha stood on tiptoe, trying to see the horses from her ground-level position on the track. "Too bad I don't have my binoculars," she murmured. She settled back on her heels to wait for the horses to come around the far turn.

In less than a minute she heard the distant thunder of hooves. The thunder became a roar as the horses raced into the far turn, heading for home. Prospector's Whimsy was still on the lead. But he seemed to be tiring—Snowy Gulch and Magenta Mile were gaining on him with every stride!

"Come on, Prospector!" Samantha cried, caught up in the excitement of the race.

Prospector's Whimsy's ears pricked forward, as if he saw the wire rushing toward him. Then they swept back to listen to his jockey.

In one fluid motion the gray colt switched leads and dug in deeper. He found a fresh burst of speed, increasing his lead to four lengths . . . to five as he flew down the stretch!

Samantha watched, gripping the fence tightly with her hands. *I wish so much I could ride a horse like that,* she thought fervently. She imagined herself in the tiny racing saddle, looking through Prospector's small, well-shaped ears as the Thoroughbred beneath her pounded for the finish.

"Prospector's Whimsy is still under a hand ride," the announcer called. "And there's the wire! Prospector's Whimsy wins it by three."

"Wow!" Samantha clenched her trembling hands. "Good run, boy!"

An old man standing next to her at the rail looked over at her. "So you know something about horses, eh, young lady?"

"A little." Samantha felt a sudden wave of depression. She might dream of riding, but her dad would never let her. Samantha sighed. In fact, she'd better go find him before he came looking for her.

"Well, don't be discouraged." The old man winked. "Someday soon you'll be out there with the horses—I can tell."

Samantha tried to smile, but she was sure the old man was wrong. *Mom would want me to ride,* she thought as she walked around the track to the barns. *But I can't even ask Dad.*

Ian was standing in one of the shed row aisles, talking to Arthur Gilman, a leading trainer at Hollywood Park. Her dad looked tense.

"Samantha, this is Mr. Gilman," Ian introduced them. "My daughter, Samantha."

Mr. Gilman barely nodded, then turned his back on her to continue his conversation with Ian. "You'll find that Wild Folly is still a little sore, but it's nothing much."

Mr. Gilman must be dumping his hurt horses on Dad, Samantha thought.

"All right, I'll take care of it," Ian said dismissively to Mr. Gilman.

Samantha had to hide a smile. Nobody could push her dad around.

Mr. Gilman looked surprised, then annoyed. "Good," he said. "Then we need not discuss this further." He walked off down the aisle.

Ian gazed after him with a wry smile. "I'm not sure I handled that too well," he said.

"Who cares about him? Which horses are you going to be training, Dad?" Samantha asked.

"Some pretty good ones," Ian replied. "Come on—let's take a look."

I wish Dad could get a chance to train stakes horses again, Samantha thought. *We should never have left Gulfstream.* Allowance horses were a big step up from claimers, but they weren't the top racers.

"This is Lucky Find," Ian said, moving to the stall of a brown horse with a broad blaze. "Arthur Gilman just ran him in a stakes and he came in fifth. He might belong in allowance company."

"Huh." Samantha studied the horse. He had a sweet expression, and he was a beautiful animal—nearly all the horses at Hollywood Park were. But he didn't have that showy presence, that fire in his eyes she associated with true champions.

Ian moved on to the next horse, a big black. "Wait,

Dad," Samantha called. She was afraid to ask him, but she just had to. "Can I help with the horses?"

Her dad's forehead furrowed. Samantha's heart sank as she realized she knew what the answer would be even before he spoke. "Sammy, please don't start talking about that again. I've thought a lot about your future, and I just don't think a career around horses is a good idea. I think you should find other interests."

"You have a career around horses!" Samantha cried.

Ian sighed. "But this is all I know how to do, Sammy. I can't change now, or I might. Do you realize how hard it is for me to go on without your mother, as if nothing happened?"

But I can't change either, Samantha cried silently. *And I don't want to do anything else.* She stared at her dad, willing him to understand. But Ian's expression stayed the same—concerned and gentle, but absolutely firm.

Samantha heard an uneven clopping sound on the concrete aisle. Turning, she saw a limping horse being led back to its stall. "Who's that?" she asked, grateful for an excuse to break the long silence between her and her father.

The dark brown horse was tall, with good lines. He had four flashy white stockings, a luxurious deep brown mane and tail, and a broad blaze shaped like a comet, with a star at the top. Despite his obvious pain, he was obediently following his handler as best he could.

"That's Bow Tie," Ian said. "He came in dead last in a race last week. His running days are over."

"So what's going to happen to him?" Samantha asked anxiously.

Ian shrugged. "I'm not sure. That's his trainer leading him, Mack Bradley. You can ask him."

"Maybe I will." Samantha was a little afraid to talk to some of the trainers, but Mr. Bradley looked kind. Plus she felt drawn to the horse.

"I've got to order some supplies before the end of the day," Ian said. "Do you want to come with me?"

"No, I think I'll look around here and finish meeting the rest of our horses." Samantha hoped her dad wouldn't insist on staying with her.

"Okay." Ian nodded. "But Sammy, remember. Don't go anywhere near them until I'm here to supervise."

"I won't," Samantha said reluctantly. As soon as her dad had left, she approached Mr. Bradley. He had just let Bow Tie into his stall.

"Hello there," Mr. Bradley said cheerfully. He was a short, slim man in his forties. Samantha thought he might be a former jockey.

"Hi," she said timidly. "I'm Samantha McLean."

"Mack Bradley." Mr. Bradley extended a hand, and Samantha shook it.

Bow Tie leaned over his stall door. Mr. Bradley

laughed. "You want to be introduced, too?" he asked. "Well, Bow Tie, meet Samantha McLean."

"Hi, boy," Samantha said softly. She stretched out a hand to the tall colt.

Bow Tie bent his dark brown neck over the door and deeply sniffed her hand. Then he slowly moved his nose up to her shoulder, then her hair.

Samantha stood quietly, letting the colt check her out. At last he dropped his nose back to her hand and gently nibbled on it.

"He likes you," Mr. Bradley said. "He doesn't take to everybody, that's for sure. That may be why he had so much trouble under different jockeys on the track. But we'll never know now—he's injured for good."

"So what will you do with him?" Samantha asked.

Mr. Bradley shrugged. "We'll try to sell him to someone who will recondition him as a pleasure horse. I don't think he's got a future as a jumper—his knees are shot. But he'd make somebody a nice riding horse."

Samantha looked quickly back down the aisle. Her dad had disappeared. "May I go in the stall?"

"Sure," the trainer said. "Bow's in pain, so be careful. But I think he'd like a little sympathy."

Samantha stepped into the stall. Bow Tie looked at her suspiciously. He moved toward the back of his stall. "It's okay," she soothed. "I'm not going to hurt you."

Stroking the colt's shoulder, Samantha ran her

hand down his left front leg. Bow Tie flinched. "Steady, boy." Samantha kept her touch very light.

The colt sniffed her hair again, then relaxed. He seemed to realize she was trying to help him.

Samantha winced as she gently massaged Bow Tie's swollen knees. *Somebody really did a job on you,* she thought. She doubted if it had been Mr. Bradley. Probably the colt's owners had overraced him.

Mr. Bradley looked over the stall door. "You want to buy him?" he asked.

Samantha was startled. She slowly stood up. "Oh—no, I can't."

"Why not? Your dad's a trainer. His kid should have a horse." Mr. Bradley looked at her quizzically.

Samantha stared at the ground, wondering what to say. She couldn't tell someone she'd just met the whole complicated story of why she wasn't even allowed near horses. "I just can't," she said finally.

"That's too bad." Mr. Bradley shook his head. "If Bow was yours, you could take care of him. I don't have much time for him—I have to concentrate on the racehorses. But it'd be nice if somebody would ice his knees a couple of times a day and bring down that swelling. Otherwise, I don't know if anybody will buy him."

"Then what will happen to him?" Bow Tie had edged over to Samantha in the stall. With a little sigh, he put his head into her arms, as if he had decided to trust her absolutely.

114

"He'll be put down, I guess."

"You can't!" Samantha burst out.

The trainer looked at her in surprise. "It's not my decision. The owner said if he doesn't sell in a month to six weeks, we'll have to look at other options."

Samantha thought fast. She could never let a horse as nice as this be put down. Bow Tie looked at her with his big brown eyes, as if he knew she was his last hope.

"Can I help you take care of his knees?" Samantha asked. "I'd brush him, too."

"That'd be great." Mr. Bradley beamed. "I can tell you know your way around horses."

"There's just one problem." Samantha drew a deep breath. "My dad can't know."

The trainer frowned. "Why not?"

"Because . . ." Samantha let out a big sigh. "Well, he'd worry if he knew. But he wouldn't *really* mind." Samantha crossed her fingers behind her back. That definitely wasn't true. But she knew that taking care of Bow Tie was a matter of life and death. "He's such a nice horse," she pleaded. "I want him to find a good home."

"Okay," said the trainer at last. "I think he's a good horse, too. He certainly won a lot of races for me. I owe him one."

"Thank you!" Samantha grinned.

"Thank *you*. I just hope all your work isn't for nothing."

"It won't be," Samantha said firmly.

115

"Let's talk tomorrow." Mr. Bradley turned to go. "We'll figure out what to do. Right now I've got to get out to the track."

"Did you hear that, boy?" Samantha happily asked the colt. Bow Tie huffed out a little sigh, as if he were relieved to have things settled, too. *I bet I can make him look good enough for somebody to buy,* Samantha thought confidently, rubbing the colt's neck. *But I'd better get out of this stall before Dad comes back.*

She had just shut the stall door when she heard her dad's voice. "Samantha?"

Samantha jumped back in fright, but Ian didn't seem to notice. "Let's go," he said.

"Go where? Our new house?" Samantha hurried after her dad. Bow Tie whinnied, but Samantha didn't dare turn around. *I've really got to be more careful,* she warned herself. *Being in Bow's stall might seem like a little thing—but it's not. Dad really thinks that if I won't stay away from horses, I belong with my grandparents.*

"I haven't found a place for us to rent yet," Ian said. "Let's get a paper and check out the ads. We need to be close to the track."

"Okay." That sounded good to Samantha. The closer they were to the track, the more time she could spend with Bow Tie.

Ian pulled up to a chain restaurant and bought a paper. Samantha ordered hamburgers and sat down across from him with their tray.

"Let's enroll you in school this afternoon after we find a house," Ian said, studying the paper.

"Do we have to?" Samantha asked.

Her dad looked up. "Why not? Don't you want the chance to meet some other kids?"

"It's so near the end of the school year." Samantha shrugged. "I don't want to go for just two weeks." If she didn't have to go to school, she could take care of Bow Tie full-time.

"But Sammy, won't you be lonely if you don't go to school?" Ian pressed.

"I'll meet people at the track." Samantha tried to sound convincing. She probably wouldn't meet anyone her age there, but that was okay. Bow would keep her busy enough.

"Well . . . I suppose you have a point," Ian said slowly. "But Sammy, I want you to have fun. It's so important to me that you're happy."

"I will be," Samantha promised. *As long as you don't find out what I'm doing,* she thought guiltily.

9

"SO WE'RE JUST A FIVE-MINUTE DRIVE FROM THE TRACK,"
Ian said, looking around their rental house that afternoon. "We were lucky to find this place."

Samantha dropped her suitcase in the living room
with a thud. "Yeah, it's . . . um . . ." She glanced
around the unfurnished space, searching for something positive to say. "It's really big," she finished.

Samantha wandered into one of the bedrooms. The
house had three bedrooms, with a living room,
kitchen, and family room. The front windows looked
out on a busy street.

"What will we do with the extra bedroom?"
Samantha murmured. "We don't have enough people
to fill up this house." She sat down on the wood floor,
suddenly depressed. She tried to console herself with
the thought of spending more time with the horses.

Her dad walked into her room. "Looks a little empty," he said. "Kind of Japanese style, with no furniture."

Samantha tried to smile.

"Let's go shopping and fix this place up," her dad said. "Then we can get settled in."

"Okay. Um, Dad—then I guess we should go back out to the barn?" Samantha asked, getting up.

"We can go this afternoon, after our shopping trip." Ian paused in the doorway and frowned. "I'm not sure it's good for you to be getting this wrapped up in the barn again."

"It's not that. It's just . . . well, you never showed me the rest of your horses," Samantha said in a rush.

Her dad's face cleared. "That's right," he said. "I'll introduce you to them. But Sammy, please remember to stay away from all the horses unless I'm around."

"Okay," Samantha said automatically. *He's got to change*, she thought desperately as she followed her dad out of the house. *I don't want to keep lying to him.*

One afternoon two weeks later Samantha walked onto the track backside, then stopped to catch her breath. She had run almost the whole way from her house to the track, anxious to see Bow. "This would be a good beach day," she murmured.

It was almost June, and the air was still, hot, and

humid. The track didn't have racing that day, and the backside was quiet.

Samantha pushed damp wisps of hair out of her eyes and began to walk determinedly toward Bow's stall. Life had been so different last summer. She'd had Tiffany to hang out with and Miracle Worker to ride—and her mom. *Now Mom's gone, and I can't even get near the track with a horse*, she thought sadly.

Bow Tie whinnied happily the moment he saw Samantha approach his stall. He arched his neck over the stall door, expecting a treat. Samantha's spirits lifted at the sight of him. "You're in a good mood," she said, petting the colt's comet-shaped blaze. Bow seemed like a completely different horse these days. Samantha had managed to ice his knees three times a day without her father finding out. Handsome, affectionate, and playful, Bow didn't seem to be in pain at all anymore.

Samantha smiled as she let herself into the stall. "Let me see those knees," she said.

Bow obligingly stood still, sniffing her hair, as Samantha knelt to look at his legs. "I don't see a bit of swelling," she said with satisfaction. Samantha ran her hands lightly over the colt's knees. "No heat, either. You really are better, boy."

Bow cheerfully nudged her. Samantha stood and ran her fingers through his fine, silken coat. Over the past weeks, as she had iced his knees, brushed him, and talked to him, she'd watched with joy as he'd blossomed under her gentle treatment. She liked to imagine how pleased her mother would be with her work. The feeling was so strong, sometimes she almost thought she could hear her mother's voice.

"You look completely well," Samantha said to Bow, relief edging her voice. "But I'll ask Mr. Bradley to check you just to make sure."

Mack Bradley looked over the stall door. "Ask me what?" he said.

Samantha jumped away from Bow. Her heart was hammering. "Oh, hi, Mr. Bradley," she said. "I thought you were my dad."

"Nope." Mr. Bradley didn't say anything more. He stepped into the stall.

Mr. Bradley is really nice, Samantha thought gratefully. They had become good friends. She could tell from the sympathetic way he looked at her sometimes that he must have made inquiries about her and learned about her mother, but he never mentioned it. Samantha was thankful for that.

She tried to slow her breathing as Mr. Bradley examined the colt. *I'm so glad he wasn't Dad*, she thought. *What would I have done?*

Bow dropped his head onto Mr. Bradley's shoulder, as if he were looking at his knees, too. Samantha grinned.

Mr. Bradley stood, rubbing his hands on his jeans.

"Bow's knees look a whole lot better," he said approvingly. "I think you've got a magic touch, Sammy."

"Thanks." Samantha looked shyly at her feet. "What do you want me to do with him today?"

"I'd like to get him out of his stall," Mr. Bradley said, walking around Bow. "I've taken him out a few times, but it's not enough to get him in shape." He looked at Samantha. "Is that something you can do?"

"Today I can," Samantha said happily. She knew that her dad was out working with one of his colts. He wouldn't be back in the barns for at least an hour.

Mr. Bradley handed her a lead rope. "Be careful," he said.

"I will!" Samantha clipped the lead rope to Bow's halter, then led the colt out of the stall.

She hesitated at the doorway to the barn. *This is major*, she thought guiltily. *I won't have any excuse if Dad catches me out here, alone with a horse.*

Bow pulled impatiently on the lead line. "I know, you're dying to get out," Samantha said. She hesitated only another second, then stepped forward resolutely. *I've just got to do this*, she thought. *Nobody's going to buy him if he's been cooped up so long he goes wild the second he's out of his stall.*

Samantha circled the colt at a walk. Bow frisked at the end of the lead line, sidestepping, then burst into a trot. "None of that," Samantha ordered. "I know you feel good, but you have to mind. You don't want to stress your knees again." She pulled firmly on the lead line, signaling him to walk.

The colt tossed his beautiful head, but he followed her obediently at a bouncing walk. Samantha was glad that despite Bow's high spirits, he responded to her commands. "That's a good sign for a pleasure horse," she commented. "You're a gentleman, Bow."

Bow paced behind her, following her so closely, the lead rope was slack in her hand. Occasionally he nudged her out of sheer good will. Samantha smiled. Seeing the happy colt, she had trouble believing she was doing anything wrong.

"You might trot him," Mr. Bradley called from the doorway to the shed row. "I think he's up for that. In a couple of weeks we've got to start showing him to prospective buyers."

"Okay." Samantha glanced back at Bow. She was a little nervous about taking him at the faster pace. What if he got away from her?

Samantha clucked to the colt, cueing him to trot. Bow responded immediately, switching into a smooth, floating trot. *I bet he'd be fun to ride*, Samantha thought longingly.

"Very nice," Mack Bradley called from the barn.

Samantha pulled Bow back into a walk. "I wish I could buy you," she whispered, giving him a pat on the neck.

Bow pranced at the end of the lead line. Clearly he

didn't have a care in the world. "You are a very handsome fellow," Samantha praised.

"He's looking good!" Mr. Bradley called. "The more of that you can do, the better." He disappeared into the barn.

"Okay." Samantha stopped Bow and rested her cheek against his warm brown neck. "You need a lot of trotting to condition you, and some cantering on the longe line wouldn't hurt, either. But how can I do all that and not get caught?"

Bow swung his head in the direction of a loud, clear, woman's voice coming from behind one of the barns. "I really feel that Royal Honor peaked two days before the race. That's why his performance yesterday was poor."

"I don't agree," a man answered. He sounded angry. "You know nothing about horse racing!"

"Well, don't forget who pays the bills," the woman replied.

"Oh, no—it's the Gilmans!" Samantha whispered.

She had learned to dread the appearance of the well-known trainer, his wife, and his sixteen-year-old daughter Melanie. The Gilmans never came near Ian's horses—Samantha assumed that lowly allowance horses didn't interest them—but she seemed to run into them everywhere else.

It's as if they walk around the track all day looking for someone to pick on, she thought, frantically searching for a hiding place for herself and Bow. The Gilmans hardly ever talked to her directly, but Samantha heard them criticize her dad all the time. They'd been especially nasty after a horse of Ian's came in second in a race last week.

Samantha quickly turned Bow, hoping to make it behind the other end of the barn before the Gilmans saw them. But Bow stood motionless, staring in the direction of the voices.

Samantha tugged urgently on his lead line. "Come on, boy! We've got to get out of here!"

The colt refused to budge. He tossed his head again and waited, as if he wanted to show himself off to as many people as possible.

The Gilmans walked around the barn. Melanie Gilman frowned the moment she saw Bow. *I guess she's pretty*, Samantha thought grudgingly. Melanie had sleek, almost white blond hair, big blue eyes, and a tall, elegant figure. "What horse is that?" Melanie asked her father.

I suppose I'm invisible, Samantha thought indignantly.

"That's the old claimer Mack Bradley is trying to recondition as a pleasure horse," Arthur Gilman said, sounding bored.

"Oh, I thought he was one of Ian McLean's." Melanie looked vaguely at Samantha for a moment, as if she was trying to figure out who she could possibly be.

"No—but none of McLean's horses are any better." Mr. Gilman laughed.

125

"That horse looks terrible," Melanie said. "All flabby and gangly. No one would buy him."

That's what you think! Samantha was so angry at the insult to her beloved horse, she was speechless. *That's probably just as well,* she reminded herself. If she got into an argument with the Gilmans, her dad would almost certainly hear about it.

"Let's have lunch in the clubhouse," Mrs. Gilman suggested to her husband and daughter. Her voice carried clearly to Samantha.

Go eat your big, fancy lunch, Samantha thought defiantly as they walked away. *I've got better things to do!*

Samantha looked at Bow, who was still staring after the Gilmans. "You don't look awful," she said, still stinging from the other girl's remark. "Melanie is totally wrong. Besides, you're not going to be sold as a racehorse. You don't have to be in shape for the Kentucky Derby for someone to want you."

Samantha blew out a breath. She hated to admit it, but Melanie's comments worried her a little. Bow was a gorgeous horse, but Samantha knew he could be in a lot better shape. Especially with his history of knee trouble, she had to make sure he was as attractive to buyers as possible.

"Let's trot some more," she said, jiggling on the colt's lead line. "Okay? Are you done looking around?"

With a happy whicker Bow trotted after her. Samantha ran backward for a few paces, studying his gait. It was even and free. She didn't see any sign that his knees were bothering him. "That's great, boy!" she said proudly.

Samantha trotted him in several circles around the stable yard, then slowed him to a walk. "That's enough for today," she said, panting. *For me, too!* she thought. *I've been such a couch potato the past couple of months.* Bow waited patiently as Samantha tried to catch her breath.

"How'd he do?" Mr. Bradley looked up from a chart as Samantha led Bow into the barn.

"Perfectly, I think." Samantha crosstied the colt so that they could look at his legs. "How does he seem to you?" she asked anxiously.

"I don't see any problems," Mr. Bradley said, running his hands down the colt's legs.

"Good," Samantha said. "I was kind of worried about him."

Mr. Bradley looked intently at Samantha. "Why? Do you see anything wrong with him?"

"No, but I ran into the Gilmans, and they said nasty things about him." Samantha sighed, leaning against an empty stall door. "Why do they do always do that to my dad and me?"

Mr. Bradley laughed. "They're envious of your dad," he said. "After what he did with Gulfstream Waves, they know he can do anything with a horse."

"That's true." *I hope Dad trains a horse to the top again someday,* she thought.

"The cartilage in Bow's knees is badly damaged," Mr. Bradley said. "That won't change. But he's a good-looking horse. I think he'd make an excellent pleasure horse if he wasn't ridden too hard."

"I hope he finds somebody who really cares about him." Samantha walked over to the colt and rubbed his soft nose. He cheerfully bumped her hands, as if to say he had no doubts.

"Bow could probably be ridden a little at this point," Mr. Bradley said thoughtfully. "Why don't you ride him, Sammy?"

The question caught Samantha by surprise. "No, thanks," she said quickly.

"I'll bet you're a good rider," Mr. Bradley remarked. "Of course, we'd have to ask your dad's permission."

Samantha shook her head vehemently. "I just can't ride him, Mr. Bradley," she said. "Not now."

That night Samantha sat beside her dad in one of their new chairs, watching TV. The chair still smelled new, like everything else they had. *How can I get Dad to take me to the barn tonight without making him suspicious?* she wondered. Samantha desperately wanted to work with Bow.

Samantha cleared her throat. "Dad, would you drive me over to the barn?" she asked abruptly. *Sometimes the direct approach is best*, she thought.

Ian lowered the sound on the television and looked at her in surprise. "Why? It's so late."

"I want to finish cleaning some tack." Samantha hated lying to her dad, but this was an emergency. *Bow needs more exercise to look his best,* she said to herself. *If I don't get him fit enough, no one will want him and they'll put him down.* Samantha stared hard at her dad, willing him to take her to the barn.

"All right." Ian picked up his keys from the top of the TV. "But I don't want you to stay too late if you're coming to the track with me early tomorrow morning."

"I won't." Samantha planned to work with Bow in the morning, too.

A few minutes later Ian dropped her off at the backside gate, and Samantha walked slowly across the shadowy grounds toward Bow's barn. Her mouth felt dry and her stomach was tight. It wasn't that she was afraid to be at the dark track—security was tight—but she was terrified for Bow. What if he looked as bad to his owners as he had to Melanie? What if someday they just decided to sell Bow to the slaughterhouse, and she never saw him again? "I can't let that happen," she murmured, running to the barn door.

Bow was looking tranquilly over his stall door, as if he were expecting her. Samantha rushed over to him and hugged his head tight. "Bow, we have to work harder. I don't want anything bad to happen to you. I couldn't stand that."

The colt contentedly crunched a carrot she had brought, as if to say he didn't have any worries.

Samantha put him in crossties and examined him under the barn lights. A month of good food, rest, and love showed in the colt's sparkling brown coat, and his mane and tail were a rainbow of glittering brown, gold, and black lights. "You look just gorgeous," she said with satisfaction. "But we've got more work to do. Tonight I'm going to canter you on a longe line. You need more strenuous exercise, and I want to see what your gaits are like. When people come by to look at you, they'll want to know."

Bow stood quietly while Samantha brushed him, then followed her trustingly out of the barn. The night was balmy and still, with a crescent moon beginning to rise on the horizon. Samantha hesitated, taking a deep breath of the sweet, summer air, smelling of hay, grain, and horses. "I'm taking such a big chance, Bow," she said softly. "What if Dad comes back early to pick me up? If he ever catches me, he'll send me to live with my grandmother and grandfather so fast. . . ."

Bow stepped forward, as if to make up her mind for her. "Oh, I know you're worth it, boy," Samantha whispered.

At the sound of her voice Bow looked back at her. The tall colt's dark eyes shone with eagerness and affection. Samantha knew how much he depended on her.

Mom would have done this in a flash, she thought. *And I know she'd want me to.* Samantha nodded briskly and walked out into the dark stable yard with Bow.

She stopped him, then backed off a few paces. The colt started to follow. "Whoa! You wait there." Samantha raised the longeing whip she'd brought. She didn't intend to hit him hard with it, but only to use it as a pointer to give him cues.

Bow stopped, and Samantha slowly backed up until she stood at the center of the yard. She raised the whip. "Okay, boy, let's try a walk." Samantha's voice shook with tension and excitement. She lifted the whip and pointed it behind Bow's hind legs.

Bow moved off in a brisk walk, circling her. He seemed to know what to do, but then he broke into an excited trot. "Not yet," Samantha said firmly. She checked the colt with the lead line, making him walk until she was sure he was thoroughly warmed up at the slower gait.

"Now let's go faster." Samantha clucked to Bow, and he immediately responded. The colt's trot was smooth and long striding.

Samantha pulled Bow back down to a walk and looked carefully around. She and Bow were completely alone, unless she counted the skinny black cat that had just run by to the barn. It nestled in a stack of hay. "Good thing I think black cats are good luck," she murmured. "Okay, boy—let's do it. We've got to. Canter!"

Samantha flicked the whip toward Bow, asking him to canter. The colt hesitated for a stride, then broke into the rocking three-beat gait. "Perfect, Bow!" *He knows just what I want,* she thought excitedly.

Bow circled her, his canter flowing, strong, and controlled. "That's it!" Samantha cried, totally immersed in the pleasure of her success. She forgot her fears for Bow and herself.

"What's going on?" a man's voice called. "Are you all right?"

Samantha gasped. *Dad!* she thought, pulling hard on the lead rope.

Bow broke into an uncertain trot, confused by her sudden command. "Easy, boy," Samantha said. She had just recognized the track security guard. "Hi, Tim," she called back. "I'm fine!"

But I won't be if Dad catches me, she thought fearfully. She pulled Bow down to a walk, then asked him to stop.

The colt wasn't ready to end his fun. He walked on a few paces, shaking his head and snorting, as if to say, "Just a little more, please."

"I'm sorry, boy." Samantha's knees were still shaking. "That's it for us tonight." She looked over the colt one last time. In the moonlight Bow's dark silhouette, from his fine head to the sweep of his straight back and slender legs, was regal.

Samantha sighed. "You have beautiful gaits, Bow. I

sure saw that tonight. Your new owner's going to like riding you."

The next morning Samantha sat on her packed suitcase, still shaking her head in disbelief. On the drive back from the track the night before, her dad had told her they were moving to the track in Del Mar, farther south in California—today.

"Are you ready, sweetheart?" Ian walked into the living room.

"As ready as I'll ever be," Samantha said unhappily. *How can you do this to me?* she thought.

Ian squatted down beside her. "Sammy, I know it's hard to move again," he said gently. "But you must have known we'd have to go soon—the meet's almost over here. I got a call last night while you were at the barns, from one of the new owners I'll be working for at Del Mar, asking me to come right away. I figured we could leave on such short notice since you don't have school."

"I know." Samantha looked away. She knew she should have been better prepared for this possibility. Her dad was a trainer, and that job involved a lot of moving around. *But why couldn't he have waited just a little longer!* she thought.

Ian looked troubled. "This move might actually be good for you. It worries me that you don't have any friends, honey."

133

I do have a friend—Bow! Samantha cried silently. *What's going to happen to him when I'm gone?*

"I'm all right," she got out. "I'll just put my stuff in the truck." She didn't dare let her dad see how upset she was.

"Let's talk for a minute." Ian touched her arm. "Sammy, I don't want you to shut yourself off from people—from me."

Samantha looked up into her dad's concerned face. "I'm not," she said.

"I know you still miss Miami." Ian sighed. "I do, too, so very much."

"Then let's go back there—just for a visit!" Samantha said quickly.

Ian hesitated. "Sweetheart, I don't think that would be good for you right now. I don't think you should dwell on the past."

Samantha shook her head. *How can I forget Mom?* she thought, even though she knew her dad wasn't asking her to do that.

"Del Mar really is a beautiful town, right on the ocean," her dad coaxed. "It's a great place to spend the rest of the summer."

But what's going to happen to Bow without me? Samantha thought frantically. She buried her face in her hands, overwhelmed. *I've got to be a good sport,* Samantha told herself, but she just couldn't. She wouldn't be able to tell Bow where she went. He'd just have to wonder—and not understand.

"Give it a try, anyway," Ian said softly.

Samantha nodded mutely. *What choice do I have?* she wondered. "Can we stop at the track for a minute?" she asked. "I want to say good-bye to Mr. Bradley." *To Bow,* she added sadly to herself.

Her dad squeezed her hand. Samantha hoped he didn't remember that Mr. Bradley was out of town today. "Sure, we'll stop," Ian said. "You and Mack Bradley really hit it off, didn't you?"

Samantha nodded, not trusting herself to speak.

On the drive to the track her dad talked more about Del Mar, but Samantha barely heard. *How am I going to get near Bow?* she thought desperately.

Ian parked at the track. "While we're here, I'm going to tidy up a few loose ends," he said. "I'll come find you in a minute."

"Okay!" Samantha ran toward Bow's barn.

The track was bustling with racehorses, trainers, and grooms as the horses were readied for the afternoon races. Samantha carefully picked her way around the excitable horses.

"Bow?" she called anxiously as she hurried down the aisle in his barn. She needed so much to see the beautiful, cheerful colt, if only for one last moment.

Bow's stall was empty. Samantha's hand flew to her mouth. "But . . . where is he?" she asked. She stood frozen in place, tears choking her throat. "Bow," she whispered as images of the sprightly, sweet-tempered colt filled her mind. "Please, please don't be gone."

135

She heard a loud, familiar whinny from the stable yard. Samantha jerked up her head. "Bow?" she cried.

Samantha tore out of the barn. Walking in the stable yard, under English saddle, was the elegant brown colt. A young brunette woman expertly guided him at a posting trot. Bow twisted his head as he passed Samantha, trying to see her, but the young woman straightened him out.

Samantha's gaze traveled from the rider to the graceful colt to a green two-horse trailer parked near the barns. *She's come for him,* Samantha realized. She felt a weird mix of emotions—heartfelt relief that the colt would live, but terrible pain at the thought that now she really was losing him.

Without thinking, Samantha walked out into the yard and looked up at the young woman. *I need to tell her about Bow,* she thought numbly. But Samantha couldn't speak past the lump in her throat.

"Yes?" The rider pulled up the colt. She looked puzzled.

"I just wanted you to know . . ." Samantha cleared her throat. "That . . . Bow's a really good horse." *You seem like a nice person. Please take good care of my Bow, since I can't anymore. That's all I really wanted to say.*

Samantha turned on her heel and fled. In another second she knew she'd burst into tears.

"I know he is!" the young woman called after her. "Hey, wait—"

Samantha kept running.

Sick with grief, Samantha sat in the truck to wait for her dad. She was ready to leave—again. "Don't think about Bow," Samantha whispered, but images of him flooded her mind: of the hurt, suffering horse she'd first known, the days of carefully treating his swollen knees, and her reward—his magical canter last night under the moon. Closing her eyes, she could see the colt's sweeping, effortless motion.

But Bow was gone forever. Samantha tapped her fingers nervously on the truck door and bit down hard on her lower lip. *Maybe Dad's right—I shouldn't be around horses,* she thought. *Losing them just hurts too much.*

10

"HOME, SWEET HOME," IAN SAID WRYLY AS HE AND Samantha unpacked in mid-September in a trailer near Aqueduct, one of the big New York tracks on Long Island.

Samantha sighed and set down her suitcase. It was getting so battered from moving around, pretty soon she'd need a new one. *At least I knew we'd be leaving Del Mar before long,* she thought. The meet was short there, just from the end of July to early September.

Ian walked by, carrying a pile of bedding. "Let's get your room set up," he said.

"Okay." Her dad always set up her room first, Samantha remembered gratefully. But she was dreading starting over in another new place. *This time I'll have to go to school,* she thought. *I bet that'll be hard.*

She tossed a stack of T-shirts on top of the bureau.

She hadn't really had much fun at Del Mar. It was a beautiful track, and the ocean and beaches were gorgeous. But her dad was worried about her because of all the moves, and he'd really kept an eye on her. Samantha hadn't been able to spend any quality time with the horses there. Finally her dad had relented and let her groom one of his horses, but it was nothing like the thrill of really working with Bow and accomplishing something. "Or riding," Samantha murmured.

Ian stepped inside her bedroom. "Let's go over to the school and register you," he said. "You can start today if you want."

"Do I really have to go?" Samantha looked at her fingernails.

"Of course—why wouldn't you?" Ian stared at her in surprise.

"I didn't in Hollywood Park," Samantha reminded him. "Why don't we go to the track first?" *That'll put it off for a little while,* she thought.

"Not until we get you settled in school," her dad said firmly. "What's the matter, Sammy? It'll be nice for you to be around kids again instead of hanging out with old trainers and jockeys."

Samantha shrugged. "I liked the old trainers and jockeys," she mumbled.

Ian jingled his truck keys. "Let's go."

Samantha saw her dad watching her closely on the drive to the school. She crossed her arms and looked out the window.

Ian registered her in the school office. The secretary smiled kindly as she reached across her desk and handed Samantha her schedule of classes. "Here you are," she said. "Since this is a big school, I've arranged for another student to show you around."

Samantha smiled back weakly.

"Sounds good, huh, sweetheart?" her dad asked.

Samantha nodded and tried to look enthusiastic.

"Ride the bus home," he said. "I'll see you tonight."

Samantha dug her heel into the linoleum floor as she waited for her student guide. *Just don't expect anything,* she warned herself. *The kids here may not like strangers.* The door to the office opened, and a dark-haired girl walked in.

"Alicia Stevens, this is Samantha McLean," the secretary said. "Alicia's in seventh grade, too. You're in several of the same classes."

Samantha stood up. "Hi," she said. Alicia was shorter than she was and had big brown eyes. She wore her hair in a French braid.

"Hi," Alicia replied with a friendly smile. Samantha found herself smiling back. She dared to hope that she had found a friend.

"Come on—I'll show you around our wonderful school," Alicia said wryly.

As they walked down the hall Samantha noticed that Alicia was wearing riding clothes. "Do you ride?" Samantha asked. She was sure she knew the answer.

Alicia laughed. "That's *all* I do—except when I'm

140

stuck at school. My mom's a trainer at Aqueduct, and we have a farm with four Thoroughbreds. How about you?"

"Well . . . my dad's an assistant trainer at the track," Samantha offered. She didn't want to talk about her own riding experience.

"You must be a great rider, then." Alicia pointed at a classroom door. "That's our first-period class—math. Mr. Harrington, the teacher, is old and weird and totally into numbers. He looks like Albert Einstein, with this wild white hair flying all over the place."

Samantha giggled.

"On with the tour," Alicia said, motioning for Samantha to follow her. "There's our English classroom. About a mile on the other side of the school is the gym, where we put on shorts and T-shirts and watch Ms. Ebron, the gym teacher, teach us how to play kickball."

Samantha laughed. "You don't know how?"

"Nope. And she's been teaching us for a month. We don't pay attention to her." Alicia banged her hand along a row of lockers as they walked down the hall.

"This looks like a nice school," Samantha said. The school was big and airy, and she saw lots of students in the many classrooms. She didn't feel out of place.

"I guess it's okay." Alicia shrugged. "I'd rather be out with my horse."

"Yeah, me too," Samantha said, smiling. "But we don't have any here—just out at the track."

"Hey, why don't you come over to my house and see our horses?" Alicia asked. "Ask your parents tonight. Then you can ride the bus home with me tomorrow."

Samantha frowned. Her dad wouldn't want her to go to Alicia's if he knew that she had horses. *But he doesn't have to know*, Samantha thought rapidly. *He'll be thrilled that I'm going over to a friend's house.*

"You don't have to come tomorrow," Alicia said. "I guess you've still got a lot of unpacking to do, huh?"

Samantha shook her head. "I don't have to do it right away," she replied. "I'd like to come over to your house—my dad won't mind."

"Great!" Alicia smiled broadly. She gestured at a closed door. "Here's your third-period class, history. I'll look for you next period in kickball."

"Okay." Samantha grinned. "Maybe you can give me some pointers."

"Welcome, Samantha," said Mr. Karch, the history teacher, as she handed him her schedule. The other kids in the class all stared at Samantha, but the looks weren't unfriendly.

They must be used to seeing new kids in a big school like this, Samantha thought as she took a front-row seat. *And I've already made a cool friend who has horses!* She smiled to herself.

Samantha skipped up the steps to the trailer after school. Her dad was pushing a chair around the living room. "Oh, you already arranged furniture!" she said. "Great, Dad!"

Her dad turned. "I thought you'd be busy with school and homework, so I went ahead. How do you like it?"

"It's nice!" Samantha surveyed the layout. The big couch had deep cushions, and her dad had arranged a matching love seat and upholstered chairs across from it. The room looked comfortable and neat. *But there's always something missing, no matter how hard Dad and I try*, Samantha thought. *Maybe it's the flowers Mom always had around our trailer in Miami. I don't know.*

Her dad gave her a weak smile. "Did you like your classes?" he asked.

Samantha nodded, noticing how tired her father looked. He'd been out on the track since five, before driving her to school. "They were good," she said, setting her backpack on the couch. She'd especially liked the classes she shared with Alicia. They'd teamed up in kickball for a smashing victory, clowning around and laughing the whole time at the frustrated gym teacher, who had ordered them repeatedly to settle down. "I made a new friend," she added.

"That's wonderful, Sammy." Ian smiled warmly.

"She invited me over to her house tomorrow—I could just ride home with her on the bus. Is that okay?" Samantha asked in a rush.

"Of course! You can have kids over here, too."

"Sure," Samantha said noncommittally. *But it wouldn't be as much fun since we don't have horses*, she added to herself. Her dad looked so happy for her, Samantha felt a stab of guilt. *He wouldn't be happy if he knew about Alicia's horses!* she thought.

"Let's go get something to eat," Ian suggested. "Are you hungry?"

Samantha nodded. "I always am." Her father's face, so full of loving concern, suddenly was very dear to her. "You're the best, Dad!" she said, running to his open arms.

Ian kissed the top of her head. "Thanks, sweetheart. I sure always want the best for you. I couldn't ask for a better daughter."

Samantha felt her happiness dim a little. *You wouldn't think that if you knew how much I lie to you*, she thought, stifling a sigh. *But what can I do?*

The next afternoon Samantha got off the bus with Alicia at her stop. "My house is just down this lane," Alicia said.

Samantha sniffed the fresh, dry air, tinged with woodsmoke. The trees were just beginning to turn their fall colors, and the leaves were a colorful green and yellow against the overcast sky. "It's really fall here, isn't it?" she asked as they walked down the lane.

"Almost," Alicia replied. "I like fall, except winter comes afterward. It gets freezing cold here in the winter, and sometimes we have a lot of snow. I hate it when I can't ride."

Samantha looked up at the immense, shady maples that hung over the lane. "I've never been up north in the fall or winter," she said. "I don't really know what seasons are like."

"You're from Miami, right?" Alicia asked.

"How did you know?" Samantha looked at her in surprise.

Alicia shrugged. "My mom talked to your dad yesterday. I guess someone took him around to meet everybody at the track." Alicia pointed. "There's my house."

"Wow!" Samantha gasped. Up ahead she could see an enormous gray colonial house with white trim, surrounded by a long yard sprinkled with big trees. Behind it was a small red barn. To the left was a training track.

In the paddock next to the barn four exquisite Thoroughbreds grazed: a black, two chestnuts, and a gray that looked almost white. "Those are our horses," Alicia said. "They're all retired from the track. The horses my mom trains are over at Aqueduct."

"This is fantastic," Samantha breathed. "It's a real home," she added wistfully.

"Thanks." Alicia smiled. "Do you want to get a snack in the house, then we'll go see the horses?"

"No, I want to see the horses first." Samantha was already walking toward the paddock.

"Good choice," Alicia said approvingly.

The horses had moved over in front of the barn. Alicia stopped off in the tack room to pick up some carrots, then stepped through one of the big box stalls to the paddock. She handed half of the carrots to Samantha.

Samantha grinned as the four horses swirled around them, urgently questing for the treats. "What are their names?" she asked.

"Dream of Gold is the chestnut, Royal Beauty's the light gray, Paradise Won is the other chestnut, and Blackie is—guess what—the black horse." Alicia grimaced. "My mother named him. She thinks she's funny. I mean, yeah, he's black—but what kind of a name is that?"

"He's beautiful, though." Samantha couldn't take her eyes off the horses.

"Which one do you want to ride?" Alicia asked.

"Oh—none of them." Samantha kicked at the dirt with her foot.

"What?" Alicia looked stunned.

"I'm not allowed," Samantha explained. "I'll just watch you," she added. She'd known Alicia would ask her to ride, and every bit of Samantha yearned to be on one of those beautiful Thoroughbreds. But she didn't dare risk it. The consequences would be utterly disastrous if her dad caught her riding.

Alicia stared at her. "Your father is a Thoroughbred trainer, and you aren't allowed to ride?"

146

"No," Samantha whispered.

"Oh, I get it," Alicia said quietly. "Your mom."

Samantha felt the color drain from her face. *That's the first time anybody's talked about Mom's death since the funeral, except for Dad.*

"My mom told me this morning. She said I should know before you came over. It must be awful," Alicia said sympathetically.

"Thanks." Samantha straightened her shoulders. *I'm glad she knows*, Samantha thought suddenly. *Now everything's out in the open.*

She looked back at the horses. They were standing in a perfect row next to the gate, as if they were waiting for her to choose one.

Samantha took a deep breath. "I changed my mind," she said. "I do want to ride. I guess I can after all."

"Fantastic!" Alicia grinned. "Why don't you ride Dream of Gold?"

"Sounds good." Samantha walked over to the gate and held out a carrot to Dream of Gold. "Your name fits you," she murmured. Dream of Gold's golden coat gleamed in the afternoon sun. His thick mane and tail were a darker bronze.

Dream of Gold seized the carrot from her hand and greedily munched. "Pretty good, huh?" Samantha asked, rubbing his forehead.

"He didn't even like carrots when we got him last month from the track," Alicia said. "I guess he got used to being spoiled pretty fast."

"He's gorgeous." The chestnut colt had two satiny stockings on his hind legs and a broad blaze. He had a lively, almost mischievous expression in his dark eyes.

Alicia nodded. "Dream did okay on the track."

"Are you sure you don't want to ride him?" Samantha asked.

"No, that's all right. These other guys aren't slouches, either," Alicia said. "Besides, I can ride Dream anytime. You should ride the horse you want."

"Well, okay." Samantha led Dream of Gold into the barn and quickly brushed him and tacked him up. She tried not to dwell on the fact that Alicia's mom might see her riding, then mention it to Ian at the track.

"Where do you want to go?" Alicia asked, walking over with Paradise Won, the other chestnut Thoroughbred. "There are a lot of trails out here. I guess it depends how much time you have."

"My dad's not coming to pick me up for a couple of hours," Samantha said. "He's going over to Aqueduct."

"Good!" Alicia grinned. "We can get in a long ride."

The girls led the horses out of the barn. Samantha easily jumped into the saddle from a mounting block. *Wow,* she thought, a huge grin involuntarily breaking across her face. *I'm really on a horse again!* The reins felt smooth and supple in her hands, and Dream's small movements beneath her as he shifted his weight were familiar and exciting all at the same time.

Samantha looked between Dream's ears, enjoying the view from high up on a horse's back. *This is so wonderful!* she thought in delight.

"So?" Alicia said. "Where to?"

Samantha's eyes were drawn to the training track. She hadn't ridden on a track since last spring. *Who knows when I'll get a chance to again?* she thought. "How about the track?" she asked.

"Sounds good," Alicia said. "Just hang on to Dream. I'm not sure he always knows he's a *retired* racehorse."

"I will." Samantha looked quickly around, then urged Dream toward the track with her legs.

The colt didn't have to be asked twice. With a snort he marched briskly toward the track, which was situated on a small rise and surrounded by trees.

"Hey, what's the hurry?" Alicia asked, laughing as she trotted up beside Dream on Paradise Won.

Dream passed the row of trees and walked onto the track. Samantha breathed a sigh of relief—now no one could see them. "I just can't wait to get started!" she said, but she hesitated, holding Dream at the edge of the track. *This is my first ride since Mom's accident,* she thought. *Can I really do it, or will I make another terrible mistake?*

"Let's go, then!" Alicia walked Paradise off down the track.

Samantha stared after her. Dream tried to follow, but Samantha expertly pulled him up. The colt's ears flicked back, listening for her orders. Suddenly confidence flowed through Samantha's veins. "I can make him mind," she murmured. "I'll get the best from him. Just like I did with Bow!"

She let Dream's reins out a notch. The spirited racehorse immediately marched after Paradise, his neck arched against Samantha's restraint. But he was minding beautifully. *I know what I'm doing,* Samantha thought proudly as they caught up to Paradise.

The girls walked the horses along the half-mile track, then trotted them. "They should be warmed up by now—let's gallop," Alicia suggested.

Samantha hesitated again. She could feel the coiled strength of the eager Thoroughbred beneath her. The colt's muscles were still well conditioned from racing, and he flung up his head and sidestepped. He wanted to run!

Without another thought Samantha let up on Dream's reins and crouched forward over the colt's neck. In an instant Dream bounded into a gallop, flying around the turn ahead of Paradise.

"Cool!" Alicia shouted. "Dream hasn't forgotten how to race!"

The next moment Samantha knew for sure he

hadn't. Golden Dream switched leads and roared down the stretch, breathing fire!

Samantha felt a flash of pure, stark fear. *What if I can't stop him?* she cried silently.

Paradise Won shot up on their outside. "Race you," Alicia yelled.

Alicia's challenging tone snapped Samantha out of her fears. *Dream's not out of control—he's just running his fastest!* she thought. "Fine, but you're not going to win!" she shouted back.

Leaning over Dream's neck, she kneaded her hands into his neck, asking him for speed. The colt gladly responded, surging into the lead by a length as the horses rounded the first turn. Samantha laughed aloud as she glanced over her shoulder to check their rival's position. Alicia was beaming as she urged her mount on, closing to half a length on Dream. The thunder of the colts' hooves pounded in Samantha's ears.

"Come on, Dream!" Samantha cried. The colt gamely responded, digging for ground, his hooves plunging deep into the track. The wind stung Samantha's eyes as she crouched even further over the colt's neck.

"This is so great," she breathed. As she thrilled to the sensation of galloping on a Thoroughbred again, Samantha felt closer to her mother than she had since her death. Briefly closing her eyes, Samantha imagined that her mother was riding beside her, encouraging her with a warm smile. *When I feel this good, I know Mom is happy for me*, she thought. *I could ride like this forever!*

"*Samantha, what are you doing?*"

Samantha jerked her head around. "Oh, my God," she gasped. "Dad!" She sat back in the saddle, her mouth dry with fear.

Responding to Samantha's movement, Dream dropped off the pace. Paradise shot by them in a second, but losing the race was the least of Samantha's worries now. Feeling utterly defeated, she pulled Dream to a walk, then turned and trotted him back to the gap.

Ian was gripping the rail. His knuckles were as white as his face. "*Get off that horse this second!*" Her dad's voice shook.

Despite her own fear, Samantha felt bad for him.

Alicia galloped up to Samantha and quickly stopped Paradise Won. "Give Dream to me," she said. "I'll pony him back to the barn."

From her friend's guilty expression, Samantha realized that Alicia had known all along that Samantha wasn't allowed to ride. She tried to smile thanks at her friend for the support.

Samantha slowly dismounted from Dream. She could hardly bear to hear what her dad would say.

Ian handed Dream's reins to Alicia. "I'm Sammy's father," he said. "You must be Alicia."

Alicia nodded. "I'm sorry, Mr. McLean."

"So am I," Ian said quietly. He turned to Samantha. "Sammy, let's go home. We'll talk on the way."

"See you tomorrow at school, Sammy," Alicia said sympathetically.

"Thanks for having me over." Samantha looked at the ground. *And for letting me have such a wonderful ride,* she added to herself.

Ian was silent on the drive back to the trailer, but Samantha could tell from his creased brow that he was thinking hard. She slumped in the seat and pressed her forehead against the window. A light rain had begun to fall, and rolling mist shrouded the farmer's fields, buried under the stalks and husks from last summer's corn. *Dad's going to send me away,* she thought desperately.

Ian parked the truck in front of the trailer, but he didn't get out.

"What are you going to do to me?" Samantha blurted, blinking back tears.

Her dad shook his head and gazed at her. "Oh, Sammy. How long has this been going on?"

"How long has what been going on?" Samantha asked nervously. Had he guessed about Bow Tie and Satin Doll? If so, she was really in deep trouble.

"You riding." Ian's voice was sad.

"Today was the only time." Samantha bit her fingernails.

Her dad fell silent again. Samantha couldn't bear the suspense. "Please don't send me away," she burst out. "Are you that mad at me?"

Ian sighed. "Sammy, I'm not mad. I'm disappointed that you disobeyed me. You just don't seem to understand that I want you to be very careful around horses for your own good. Maybe you would be better off with your grandparents—"

"No!" Samantha said fiercely. "I want to stay with you!" She looked down at her hands. "I won't ride anymore at Alicia's. I promise. I . . . I don't even have to see her anymore."

Ian looked pained. "Sammy, I don't want to punish you. . . ."

Then don't, Samantha thought in agony. *Staying away from the horses is punishment enough!*

"I just want what's best for you. Of course you can still see Alicia." Ian smiled wearily. "And if I sent you away, it would break my heart. But leave the horses alone."

"I will," Samantha promised quickly.

"I came by Alicia's early because I have some news," Ian said tentatively.

"What?" Samantha could tell by her dad's tone that he didn't think she'd like it.

"Come on inside." Ian got out of the truck. "Let's get a drink and a snack, and then we'll talk."

Samantha followed her dad into the trailer. *I'm so glad Dad's letting me stay*, she thought. But she couldn't help remembering her glorious gallop on Dream of Gold, with the wind in her face and the powerful, eager horse beneath her. *I'd give almost*

anything to feel that way again, she thought wistfully.

Ian got them each a soda from the refrigerator and
opened a bag of pretzels. Samantha sat across from
him on the living room couch and waited warily. "So
what's your news?" she asked.

"Well . . ." Her dad hesitated. "We're not going to
be here much longer. In a month or two we'll leave
for the Finger Lakes track."

Samantha stared at him, devastated. Finger Lakes
was a small track way north in upstate New York.
"Why . . . why would you go there?"

"A good friend of mine is going to have an operation. He needs me to help him with a horse of his."
Ian sighed. "Sammy, I don't want to leave either. I
know all this moving around isn't good for you. Here
we go again, just when you found a friend."

"I'm okay," Samantha said quickly. Inside she felt
far from okay. But by now she knew where this conversation was heading. "I *don't* want to go to my
grandparents," she said emphatically.

"Just let me think about it," her dad said softly.
"Of course I'd be terribly unhappy if you left. But
you're all I have now that your mother is gone. I can't
let anything happen to you. I'd rather you were safe
with your grandparents than out at the tracks with
me and in danger."

"I promise not to go near horses again!" The
words came out of Samantha in a wrenching cry.

Her dad looked her in the eye. "All right, Sammy, I know I have your word."

Now if only I can keep my promise, Samantha thought, gripping the arms of her chair.

11

"SO NOW I KNOW WHAT FALL IS," SAMANTHA MURMURED. She bent down to toss a pile of red and gold leaves lying under a tree just outside the Finger Lakes track. The trees were mostly bare from the storm her dad had driven through last night when they'd come up from Aqueduct. They'd arrived at Finger Lakes this morning, and Ian was inside the barns, looking at the horses he would be training.

After that frightening day at Alicia's, Samantha hadn't ridden again. But Alicia had turned out to be a real friend. "We'll do other stuff if you can't be around the horses," she'd said firmly. They'd gone to the movies and the mall together and talked about the cute boys in their class. Samantha would have really enjoyed herself—if she hadn't known that all too soon, she'd be moving on again.

A cold rain mixed with sleet had begun to fall, and Samantha shivered in her light jacket. *I've never been in winter, but I don't think I'm going to like it at all,* she thought.

"Sammy!" Ian was waving to her from the doorway to one of the barns. "Come see our horses!"

Samantha walked slowly over to him. She was almost afraid to meet them, but not for the reason her dad thought she should be. "What if I fall in love with one of them?" she murmured. "I won't be able to go near it. I know I'm out of chances with Dad."

"I'm working with seven horses," Ian said as she stepped inside the barn. He pointed to a row of stalls. "They're lined up here."

The seven horses were all looking over their half doors, but Samantha didn't see any other horses in the rest of the stalls. Her dad had clearly already gotten to know his horses, gentling them with his special touch, and now the horses were eager for more human contact. Samantha walked slowly down the aisle, touching the nose of each horse as she passed.

"Sammy, be careful," Ian pleaded. "I don't know if they bite."

Samantha ignored him. *Dad's being ridiculous,* she thought. *None of them have their ears back.*

The horses were in clean, well-kept stalls, the way her dad's horses always were. "They're all claimers?" she asked.

Ian nodded. "The horse I'm working on for my friend is a stakes horse, though."

Samantha heard a soft groan coming from the stall next to her dad's last horse in the row. She'd assumed that stall was empty.

Maybe it's a cat, she thought. Samantha looked in the stall, wrinkling her nose at the bad smell coming from it. A thin gray horse, hanging its head, stood timidly at the back of the stall. The smell was coming from the filthiest stable floor Samantha had ever seen in her life. "Dad, look at this horse!" she gasped.

Ian nodded. "I saw her," he said. "She looks terrible."

Samantha moved on to the next stall and saw another unhappy horse, every rib showing, cowering at the back. She went on to the next stall and the next, five stalls in all. Each held a frightened, abused horse.

"Whose horses are these?" she asked in horror.

"Brent Shrader's, a trainer here." Ian shook his head. "He's been warned by the track officials several times to clean up his act. I doubt if he'll be around much longer."

"Until then we've got to take care of those horses!" Samantha cried. She knew she could never bear to be around them without trying to help.

Her dad sighed. "Sammy, I'd like to, but I just don't have time to look after them every day. The horses probably won't die. . . ."

"Yes, they will, standing in that muck! They'll get

thrush!" Samantha insisted. She knew horses that had to stand in dirty, wet stalls could get soft and infected hooves, developing the condition called thrush. A horse could die from thrush if it wasn't treated. "I'm going to take care of them," she declared.

"Well . . . you can if you want, Sammy," Ian said finally. "But don't forget that even these horses can hurt you. Don't do more than clean the stalls. And don't wear yourself out—there's only so much you can do."

Samantha was only half listening. She was already walking toward the tack room door, hoping to find a wheelbarrow inside. "I'm going to start right now."

"You'll have to ask Mr. Shrader's permission before you do anything with his horses," Ian said.

Samantha stopped and turned around. "Well, where is he?"

"He's not around much," Ian said, frowning. "Obviously."

Samantha opened the tack room door. At least she could find the wheelbarrow, pitchfork, and shovel she'd need for the cleanup operation.

But to her astonishment, the first thing she saw in the tack room was a couple of cots. "What are those doing in there?" she asked.

Ian came up behind her. "I'd rented a house, but the deal fell through," he said. "I think we'll have to stay here for a couple of days. It might be fun—kind of like a camp out."

Samantha nodded slowly. "I guess," she said. One cot was under a row of saddles on posts, and another was on the other side of the tiny room, under a window. Samantha's suitcase was stowed between two tall bags of horse vitamins.

Samantha shivered as a damp breeze blew through the open door. "It's going to be cold in here at night," she said. "But it'll be nice to be close to the horses."

"I see enough of them during the day," Ian said ruefully.

"I meant the sick ones." Samantha stepped back out of the tack room and gazed down the aisle. The empty black holes above the sick horses' stalls yawned at her.

"I've got to go see my friend's horse," Ian said. "Do you want to come with me?"

"No . . . I'm going to clean up around here," Samantha said.

As soon as her father had left, Samantha walked cautiously down the aisle, looking over her shoulder. She stopped at the gray horse's stall. "Hi, there," Samantha said softly.

The unhappy mare hadn't moved since Samantha had seen her a few minutes before. She raised her head a little and took a step toward the door—then groaned in pain.

"Oh, sweetie. I'll come to you." Samantha looked anxiously up the aisle for her dad, then let herself into the stall and walked slowly toward the mare.

"You were a pretty horse once, I can tell," Samantha said soothingly, raising her hand to let the mare sniff it. "It's okay. I'd never hurt you."

Gradually Samantha worked her way along the mare's neck and shoulder, gently stroking. Then she stepped back up to the mare's head and rubbed her forehead. "I've got to see the others now," she said. "But I'll come back tomorrow."

The gray mare watched her with enormous, sad eyes. Samantha could hardly stand it. "Tomorrow I'll clean out this stall no matter what anybody says," she vowed.

An hour later Samantha walked into the tack room and sank wearily onto her cot. The poor gray mare was still groaning—Samantha knew she needed more than caresses to stop her pain. All Shrader's other horses were almost as badly off. Samantha felt exhausted and a little sick to her stomach. "Can I do enough for those horses?" she whispered. "What would you do, Mom?"

Samantha reached slowly into her suitcase and took out her mother's green velvet dress. Wrapped inside the dress was a picture of her mother. In Miami, Samantha had always kept it on her bureau, but she hadn't taken it out since she'd left.

Samantha perched the picture on the cantle of an exercise saddle right beside her cot. Running her hand gently across the saddle, she looked closely at the picture. Samantha had taken it about a month before her mom died.

I've always loved this picture, she thought. Suzanne was galloping Gulfstream on the track in Florida. Gulfstream had just changed leads in the stretch and was powering for home, as if he'd never stop running. The beautiful colt was in midair, all four hooves off the ground, almost flying. Her mom's brilliant red hair was blown loose from her neat ponytail, and her green eyes sparkled with excitement and the sheer bliss of her ride.

Samantha touched the picture's cold glass with her fingertips, willing it to come alive. *Mom*, she thought, her body shaking with silent sobs. *Mom, please, please come back. I need you so much right now.* Resting her head against the clean, well-oiled saddle, Samantha cried her heart out.

"Mr. Shrader?" Samantha hurried down the barn aisle later that afternoon.

Mr. Shrader was a tall blond man in his midthirties, about her dad's age. He was walking rapidly past the abused horses' stalls, glancing in. "Yes?" he asked. He seemed startled.

I must look like a wreck, Samantha realized. Her face felt puffy and swollen. Samantha had cried until she was exhausted, then had fallen into a troubled sleep. She'd woken up at the sound of heavy boots walking by the tack room door.

"I was wondering if you'd mind if I cleaned out

your horses' stalls," she said, trying to keep her voice calm. "And maybe brushed them."

To Samantha's astonishment, Mr. Shrader laughed. "Do what you want with them," he said. "Just don't get in my way."

"How would I do that if you're never here?" Samantha asked sharply, her temper rising.

"Hey, don't give me any lip, kid." The trainer stared at her coldly, then turned away. "It's nothing to me if you work with those horses," he called as he continued on down the aisle.

"I'm sorry," she said as politely as she could. She caught up with him in front of the stalls. "Would you mind telling me the horses' names and any problems they have?"

Mr. Shrader sighed impatiently, but he stopped and faced her.

"Just for a minute," she added.

"Okay, okay." Mr. Shrader pointed at the first horse's stall. Samantha peered around him and saw the timid, thin gray in the corner. "Josie's Girl has been off her feed since her last race two weeks ago," Mr. Shrader said. "Who knows why?"

He moved along to the next stall. "The next three—Way West, Go for Win, and Scarlet Hope—are bad bleeders. They've come out of their last couple of races just about suffocated on their own blood. Even Lasix doesn't help them."

Samantha nodded. She knew that when some

Thoroughbreds ran hard, they bled from their lungs. The drug Lasix helped some of them.

"Luck of the Draw's wind is broken." Mr. Shrader jabbed a finger at the next stall. "There's not much hope for that. Maybe somebody will buy him, but I doubt it."

Samantha leaned over Luck of the Draw's stall door. The chestnut colt shrank back.

"I haven't really decided what to do with them—they're at the bottom of the heap," Mr. Shrader said.

"The bleeders and the one that won't eat could return to racing," Samantha pointed out. "I mean, if we could help their problems."

The trainer shrugged. "Maybe," he said. "I doubt it." He turned to go.

"Just one more thing," Samantha said quickly. She knew Mr. Shrader was about out of patience.

"What now?"

"Why are they all so thin?" she asked.

"Because I don't waste any more feed on them than I have to." Mr. Shrader stared at her, clearly annoyed. "I've got other things to do. These horses are worthless. If I were you, I wouldn't waste my time on them." He walked out of the barn.

Luck of the Draw, the horse with broken wind, was coughing. Josie's Girl was still groaning softly. Samantha shook her head. "I don't know how I can take care of you guys," she said. "But I have to try. I'd better get started."

"Let's enroll you in school today," Ian said the next morning. "We can stop for breakfast first."

Samantha sat on her cot, trying to lace her riding sneakers. Her hands were so cold, she could hardly do it. The tack room was freezing.

Samantha looked up at her dad, startled. "Now?" she asked. "Can't I just start next semester?"

Ian shook his head. "Sammy, that's not a good idea. You can't hang out at the barn all day."

But I have to be here, Samantha thought. She had planned to spend the whole day helping the abused horses. They needed as much time as she had.

This morning she'd cleaned up their stalls first, then she'd tried to brush out their matted coats. But she still had a lot more to do. The horses had watched her with their big, sweet eyes, clearly grateful for the attention.

School had never seemed less important to Samantha, but she followed her dad to the truck, vowing to work twice as hard when she was at the barn.

After breakfast Ian dropped her off in front of the school. "I called the school secretary, and she's expecting you," he said. "I've got to get back to the barn. But I'll see you tonight and hear all about your day."

Samantha bit her lip. Snowflakes were swirling out

166

of the gray sky, and she felt cold, lonely, and afraid. *Don't go!* she wanted to cry, but her dad was already pulling the truck away from the curb.

Samantha walked slowly toward the school. *Be brave,* she ordered herself, but it was hard. She felt disoriented after her restless night in the tack room and the backbreaking work with the horses that morning.

In the school office she picked up a schedule of classes and walked down the hall. "What class do I have third period?" she muttered, trying to smooth out her crumpled schedule. "History? No, that was at Aqueduct. Here I've got math third period."

She found the right number for the classroom and opened the door. The teacher, a middle-aged woman, was writing on the chalkboard. When she saw Samantha, she stopped speaking and stared.

"Look at that girl!" said a chubby boy sitting in the back. He grinned at the kids sitting around him.

What's wrong? Samantha thought, startled. Then she glanced down at her clothes. She hadn't known she was going to school today, and she hadn't had time to shower or dress carefully. She had pulled on her school coat right after cleaning the stalls and now she noticed that her clothes were covered with bits of straw from cleaning the horses' stalls. Samantha touched her mane of red hair, wishing she had remembered to take out her ponytail and brush out the tangles.

All the kids in the class were gawking at her, and a few were whispering behind their hands. The chubby boy burst out laughing.

Samantha's cheeks flamed. Angry pride was all that kept her from crying.

"Um, hello," the teacher said slowly. "I'm Ms. Baxter. Are you a new student?"

"Yes," Samantha said defiantly.

"Please have a seat." The teacher managed a smile. "What's your name?"

"Samantha McLean." Holding her head high, Samantha marched to a seat and dropped her books loudly on the desk. *I don't care what they think. And I'll show them I don't care!*

12

"HEY, TRACK BRAT!"

Samantha winced, then slowly turned to face Eric Fletcher. This was only her second day of school, but she felt like she'd been suffering here a lot longer. Eric was her special tormentor. The chubby boy seemed to be in all her classes. When he wasn't insulting her in the hallways, he was whispering nasty things in her ear in class.

"Get a life, Eric," Samantha said automatically. "Tomorrow's Thanksgiving and we don't have school—what will you do if you can't bug me?"

"I've got a life," Eric retorted. "I don't live in a stall, Rumpledhairskin."

Why did I try to explain that I looked so bad yesterday because I'm staying in a tack room? Samantha wondered. *Now that story's all over the school.*

Samantha hurried into the girls' rest room to get away from Eric. *He's actually right that I live in a stall*, Samantha thought, staring at her tired reflection in the mirror. Last night Josie's Girl had been groaning so loudly, Samantha had spent the entire night with her. Samantha's soothing voice and gentle hands had seemed to ease the mare's pain a little.

Two girls were already in the bathroom, brushing their hair and fixing their makeup. Samantha vaguely recognized the taller, dark-haired girl as Susan Weber, the captain of the soccer team. The shorter, blond girl was Susan's best friend, but Samantha didn't know her name.

"So Shawn asked you out?" the blond girl asked Susan.

"Right after practice yesterday." Susan carefully brushed on mascara.

Samantha leaned against the wall. *That's the way Tiffany and I used to be*, she thought sadly. *We used to talk and laugh. . . .* Samantha sighed heavily. *That all seems like such a long time ago.*

"So I told Shawn we'd go to the movies . . . oh!" Susan stopped talking when she noticed Samantha.

The girls stared at her coldly, then walked to the door. "Let's get out of here," Susan said. "Something smells."

I do not, Samantha thought. Ian's trainer friend, Tony O'Neal, lived close to the track, and he let Ian and Samantha take showers at his house. *But there's no point in arguing with them,* she realized.

Samantha looked more closely into the mirror. "I don't look very good," she murmured. Her skin was so pale the freckles on her nose were more noticeable than usual, and she had shadows under her eyes. "Great," she muttered. "All I need is to get sick!"

By the end of the school day Samantha's fever was raging. "I'll just take an aspirin when I get home and I'll be fine," she assured herself through chattering teeth as she climbed slowly onto the bus.

Ian wasn't in the barn when Samantha arrived. She swallowed two aspirins with a glass of ice cold water from the horses' tap, then filled buckets with water for Josie's Girl and Way West. Sick or not, Samantha knew she had to care for the horses.

I don't mind, she thought. *I just wish they weren't so sick. I don't know if I'm making a difference or not.*

Samantha looked up at a chorus of soft nickers and had to smile. Not only her dad's seven horses but all five of Mr. Shrader's horses were looking out over their stall doors.

That's a switch, she thought with satisfaction.

Doggedly Samantha cleaned and filled all the horses' water buckets. Then she got the wheelbarrow out of the tack room and stopped in front of Josie's Girl's stall.

"It's clean!" she murmured. "Great!" The stall was spotless, with fresh straw piled high for a comfortable

171

bed. Samantha rolled the wheelbarrow down the aisle and looked in the other four stalls belonging to Mr. Shrader's horses. They were perfectly clean as well.

Samantha slumped on her pitchfork. "Thanks, Dad," she whispered. Her dad helped her with the other trainer's horses as much as he could.

Thank goodness he had time to help me today. The aspirin didn't seem to be helping her fever at all. Samantha's bones ached, and perspiration had broken out on her forehead.

Josie's Girl groaned softly. "Oh, girl," Samantha said, stepping inside the stall. "I know it hurts, whatever it is. I just wish I could have a vet look at you."

The gaunt gray mare dropped her head on Samantha's shoulder and let out a long sigh, as if to say, "Now I feel better."

"Yes, I'm here." Samantha hugged the thin, shivering horse. "We're both cold, but it's better now that we're together."

The mare grunted, then lay down heavily. She rolled on her side and stretched out.

Samantha took an old woolen blanket from the trunk in front of the stall and lay down beside the mare. She covered herself and as much of Josie as she could with the blanket. Samantha rested her head on Josie's warm shoulder and closed her eyes. Her whole body felt heavy.

Josie's Girl stirred and groaned again. "Shhh.

Rest," Samantha urged. She sat up and ran her hand down the mare's thin neck. "I'll take care of you. We'll make you a pretty girl again, I promise."

Josie's Girl opened her eyes, her gaze soft. "Go to sleep," Samantha whispered. "I'll stay with you. I won't leave."

The mare lifted her head a little to see Samantha better. Samantha put her arms around Josie's neck, pressing her cheek against the mare's rough coat. "Now we're okay," she said.

Josie dropped her head back on the straw, and her breathing eased a little. *She's asleep and out of her pain*, Samantha thought with relief, dropping her head back onto the mare's shoulder.

Samantha's throat was on fire, and her back, legs, and arms ached. *I'm so sick*, she thought. *I wish Mom were here to take care of me. Maybe I can dream about her for a while. That would be really, really nice.*

"Sammy? Wake up, honey. What are you doing?"

Samantha sat up with a jerk at the sound of her dad's voice. Her eyes were blurred with sleep, and she could barely see him at the stall door.

"Nothing," Samantha muttered, resting her pounding head on Josie's shoulder again. "We're just resting."

Ian opened the stall door and came inside. He put his hand to her forehead. "You're burning up with fever. Come on, let's put you to bed."

"I'm fine here," Samantha whispered. She felt so

weak, she wasn't sure if she could stand up anyway. "Why are you back from the track so soon?"

"It's so cold, the jockeys have refused to ride," Ian said. "The wind chill is minus twenty, and iceballs are smashing the jockeys' goggles. Sammy, please—let's get you in bed right away."

Something was funny about her dad's voice. Samantha's head cleared a little. "What is it?" she asked. "What's wrong?"

"Oh, Sammy . . . I'm so sorry," her dad said. He knelt beside her in the straw and squeezed her shoulders. "Come with me."

Samantha twisted in his arms. What was he talking about? He wasn't looking at her but at the quiet mare beside her. "Josie?" she asked.

The mare was sleeping beautifully, not groaning at all. But she was too still. . . .

"Oh, no," Samantha whispered. "No, sweetheart." She bent over the mare's body, tears dropping on her gray coat.

"She's out of her pain, Sammy." Her dad's voice was very sad.

You can't be dead, Samantha cried silently. *I loved you so much. And I know you loved me.*

"Poor thing," Ian said softly.

"I can't stand it," Samantha sobbed. "This isn't fair. She was so good."

"I know," her dad agreed. "But life sometimes isn't fair."

Samantha's head snapped around at the sound of someone whistling. "Mr. Shrader!" she gasped.

All Samantha's sorrow turned to rage. She forgot that Mr. Shrader was an adult and that she was so sick, she could hardly move. In one jump Samantha was at the stall door. "You killed her!" she cried. "She needed a vet, but you let her die!"

The trainer stopped whistling and stared at her. "Look, little girl—I don't need your advice on how to take care of my horses," he said.

"Yes, you do." Ian walked up behind Samantha and put a hand on her shoulder. Her dad's face was angry and stern.

"That's your opinion," Mr. Shrader said rudely.

"That's a lot of people's opinion." Ian glared at the other man. "Including the track officials'. This horse is dead because of your cruelty. I intend to help press charges."

"We'll see about that," Mr. Shrader said, but his face paled. Without another word he stalked out of the barn.

Samantha's anger collapsed, replaced by overpowering sadness. Her knees buckled and she fell to the ground.

Her dad scooped her up in his arms. "I'm so proud of you, Sammy," he said. "I've never seen anything like what you did for those horses."

"But I couldn't save her," Samantha murmured. "I tried so hard, but she died. What did I do wrong?"

"Nothing at all." Ian kissed her forehead. "I'm the one who did something wrong, letting you wear yourself out like this. But I'll make it up to you, sweetheart. I promise."

"What do you mean?" Samantha asked drowsily. She felt safe and warm in her dad's arms.

"I mean we're going to a first-class hotel tonight, and then we'll find a real place to stay," Ian said firmly.

"That's good." Samantha dropped her head onto his shoulder and closed her eyes.

"No, I mean a home, Sammy." Her dad stroked her hair. "You've worked so hard here, on some very sick horses, just because you care about horses so much. You deserve a good home, with horses that can repay your care."

"So I can be around horses now?" Samantha asked, opening her eyes. Despite the heaviness of her aching head, Samantha felt a flash of utter joy and relief.

"Yes, you can, as long as you don't ride." Her dad quickly carried her to the truck through the frosty air and set her on the seat. He carefully wrapped her in the blanket.

"I'm glad I can be with the horses again." Samantha smiled and yawned. She felt like she could sleep for a thousand years. "But you're wrong about one thing, Dad."

"What's that?" Ian looked tenderly down at her.

"Josie and the others were worth what I did for them." Samantha pulled the blanket tight around her neck. "Every bit of it."

The next morning when she woke up, Samantha could barely pry open her sticky eyes. "Where am I?" she murmured. She was lying in an enormous bed in a light, airy room. Through a picture window she could see the snowy, hilly landscape.

Her dad sat on the end of her bed. "We're in a hotel," he said.

"The horses," Samantha croaked, sitting up. "I have to take care of them."

Ian laid a gentle hand on her forehead. "Sammy, it's okay. I took care of them early this morning, and about an hour ago one of the horse rescue groups came for the rest. The track is going to prosecute Mr. Shrader for what he did to them."

"So they're all gone," Samantha whispered. She dropped back on her pillow.

"Gone, but saved—by you." Her dad kissed her forehead, then rose from the bed. "I just called room service to bring you some lunch," he said. "And when I come back, we'll order the fanciest Thanksgiving dinner ever. All the trimmings!"

"Sounds good." Samantha's mouth watered. "I think I feel better," she declared.

"Good, honey. I thought I might give you an

early Christmas present, too," her dad said casually.

"Oh, really? What?" Samantha swung her legs over the side of the bed and looked at him eagerly. Her dad always gave her great Christmas presents. "Can I have it now?"

Her dad handed her two small folders. Each had the name of an airline across it. "Merry Christmas," he said.

"Airline tickets?" Hardly daring to breathe, Samantha opened the folders and looked at the tickets. "They're to Miami!" she cried. "Oh, Dad, thank you!"

"We'll leave tomorrow and see our friends . . . and go visit your mother's grave," Ian said softly. "I'm sorry, Sammy. I should have taken you back sooner. You and I need to make peace with what's happened."

"It's okay—we're going now. We're really going." Samantha's eyes brimmed over with happy tears as she tightly clutched the tickets. *Oh, Mom, I'm coming back,* she thought. *We're going to be together again.*

"Wow, real sunshine in winter!" Joyfully Samantha spun in a circle at Ivor Stables, letting the wonderful Florida sunshine spill on her upturned face.

"It's good to be back, isn't it?" Ian asked, smiling.

"Sure is!" Samantha stopped spinning to catch her

breath. This morning they'd caught a flight out of snowy, winter-bound New York to sunshine-filled Miami. Looking at the deep green orange groves, dotted with colorful fruit, and the brilliant blue sky that she'd thought of so often, Samantha heaved a huge, contented sigh.

I want to see Mom, she thought. *She's right over there, behind that grove.*

"Ian!" called Mr. Ivor, walking down the path from the house. "It's so good to see you again. Come over here and let's talk."

"It's good to see you, too," Ian said, shaking hands with the older man.

"Hey, you don't have to stay with your dad and me, Sammy," Mr. Ivor said. "Feel free to ride Miracle or one of the other horses if you want."

"Miracle's still here?" Samantha asked in astonishment. Claimers often changed owners.

"You bet," Mr. Ivor confirmed.

"Sounds like you need to see an old friend, Sammy," Ian said. "Do you want me to come with you?"

Samantha shook her head. She could feel a big grin spreading across her face. "No, that's okay!" Samantha took off running for the barn. *I can take Miracle with me to see Mom!* she thought.

"Miracle's in the same stall," Mr. Ivor called after her.

Samantha halted her dash at the doorway to the

barn. She walked slowly down the aisle, letting her eyes adjust to the dimmer light inside.

"Miracle!" she called softly. "It's me, boy. Do you remember?"

The colt's black head popped out of his stall. Whinnying loudly, he pranced on his front feet, as if he wanted to run to meet her.

"You do remember!" Samantha hugged the happy colt's neck.

Miracle nudged her hard, almost knocking her over. "Take it easy." Samantha laughed, steadying herself on the stall door next to his.

She felt soft leather under her hand. An English saddle, with a bridle lying on top, was perched on the door. "Hey, that's your tack," she said. "Who got that out?"

Probably Mr. Ivor, she realized. Samantha stared at the tack. "Should I ride?" she asked herself. "Dad still doesn't want me to. But I want to ride out to see Mom. I have to ride out to Mom."

Samantha's hands felt as if they were moving by themselves. She led Miracle to the crossties and quickly tacked him up. No one was in sight as she led him out of the barn. "So far, so good," she whispered.

Swiftly Samantha mounted up and trotted Miracle toward the orange groves. The colt seemed to know exactly where they were going. Without being asked he turned right on her mom's favorite trail.

Samantha breathed deeply. The smell of oranges, the bright sunshine, and Miracle's steady strides were just the way she remembered. She almost felt that if she looked beside her, her mom would be riding right there. "This is where I belong," Samantha murmured.

At a fork in the trail Samantha stopped. The left fork led to the track; the right, to her mother's grave. Samantha took the left, riding up a small hill to the training track.

She looped Miracle's reins around the rail. "Wait here just a minute," she said. "There's something I have to do."

Samantha walked slowly along the track to the place where her mother had fallen. The dirt had just been harrowed, and the smooth ridges were unbroken. Samantha touched her hand to the soft ground. "I'm so sorry, Mom," she whispered.

Samantha straightened and walked back to the finish line. She scooped up a handful of the dirt there.

Miracle had dropped his head to watch her. "Come on, boy," she said, mounting up. "Let's take this back to Mom."

Her heart thumping, Samantha rode Miracle around the final turn to the grave. Ahead of her was the sunlit clearing with the simple white stone. "Hi, Mom," she said softly.

The grave was planted with vibrant red and pink pansies, but some natural vines had been allowed to creep across it. The look was wild, yet beautiful. *Just like Mom*, Samantha thought lovingly.

She slid off Miracle in front of the grave and walked slowly around it, sprinkling the dirt from the finish line. "That's what you would have wanted, isn't it, Mom?" she asked. "I'm sorry it took me so long to figure it out."

Samantha knelt in front of the grave, bending her head reverently. "I'm really back," she whispered.

As if in response, a breeze swept through the orange grove, gently rustling the leaves and swaying the fruit. Samantha touched her hand to the cool marble stone. "I love you, too," she said.

Miracle snorted softly. Samantha sat back on her heels and rubbed his nose. There in the sunshine, with the horse that her mother had known so well, too, Samantha felt healing and peace steal into her soul.

She turned at the sound of footsteps. Ian walked up beside her and put his hand on her shoulder. "Are you okay, Sammy?" he asked.

Samantha looked up at him and smiled. "I am now. I feel like Mom's forgiven me," she said quietly.

Ian looked startled. "Forgiven you? For what?"

"For what I did." Samantha swallowed hard. "For getting in Gulfstream's way on Miracle and making Mom run into that rail."

Ian knelt beside her at the grave and held her close. "Sweetheart, have you thought that all this time? You know accidents happen with horses. Your mom would never blame you for a second."

"I know." Samantha sighed deeply. But for the first time she really believed it.

"I only hope you can forgive *me*, Sammy," Ian said. "I've been so blind, moving you all over the country, trying to keep both of us from facing the past. I promise I'll make a new home for you—we owe your mom that. I bet we can do it together."

"I know we can." Samantha smiled at her dad. Now she felt sure of it.

"Come on." Ian stood and held out his hand. "Let's get dinner."

"Then can we come back?" Samantha asked softly. She took her dad's hand.

"Yes, honey," her dad promised. "As often as you want."

They stood together, facing the grave. "Good-bye, Mom," Samantha said, her voice shaking a little. She squeezed her dad's hand tight.

"Good-bye, Suzanne." Ian reassuringly returned Samantha's squeeze.

"We'll see you soon," Samantha promised. She turned to go. This time she felt all right about it. *I'm not leaving for good,* she thought.

"Did you walk him out here?" Ian asked, gesturing at Miracle.

Samantha lowered her gaze. She couldn't bring herself to tell her dad she'd ridden him. She knew her dad hadn't changed his mind about that. "Yes," she said weakly. "Miracle was already tacked up when I found him. I'd better get him back to the barn."

"I'll meet you there in a few minutes," Ian said.

Samantha took off Miracle's tack in the barn and put him back in his stall. She picked up a dandy brush and methodically ran it over his rich black coat. "There's still just one problem, Miracle," she said. "And it's a big one. Dad doesn't know that I just rode you—and that I want to ride all the time. I know it's wrong to disobey him, but I don't know what to do! I just have to ride. But I bet Dad would still send me to my grandparents if he knew." Samantha rested her cheek against Miracle's silky neck. The colt's ears twitched, as if he were listening carefully.

"Sammy, I'm not going to send you anywhere you don't want to go." Ian was standing outside the stall. He looked upset.

"Dad!" Samantha stared at him in shock. "Oh, no . . . but . . . you really won't send me to my grandparents?"

Her dad closed his eyes. "Samantha, you're all I have left. I never, ever want you to leave me—or this earth. That's why I don't want you to ride. It's the only way I know how to protect you."

"But Mom would have wanted—," Samantha began.

"Your mom died riding," Ian said gently. "I never want that to happen to you."

But I'll die if I don't ride. Samantha bit her lip and sighed. She knew her father just wasn't ready to hear that.

"I do understand that you want to be around horses. It's in your blood, just as it is for me—and was for your mother. You can groom them, longe them, and help care for them in every way—as long as you don't ride, so that I'm not scared sick." Her dad gave her a crooked smile. "Maybe, someday, when I feel braver for you, then you can have some lessons, okay?"

"Okay." *That's the best I can do for now,* Samantha realized.

Ian leaned on the stall door. "Let's talk about our next move," he said.

Samantha stiffened. *I don't want to go anywhere!* she thought. Miracle gave her a push from behind, as if he was urging her to speak up.

Her dad must have seen her expression. "I think you'll like what I have in mind," he said. "As a matter of fact, I'm sure you will."

Samantha dropped Miracle's brushes into his tack trunk and leaned on the other side of the stall door beside her dad. "I'm listening," she said.

"I've been offered a position as assistant trainer at Townsend Acres," Ian answered. "It's a top-class operation near Lexington, Kentucky."

"Ashleigh Griffen lives there!" Samantha stared at her father, wide-eyed. "She won the Breeders' Cup

Classic on Ashleigh's Wonder year before last. Townsend Acres is only the best Thoroughbred farm in the world!"

"I ran into Clay Townsend, the owner of Townsend Acres, at the fall Aqueduct meet. He mentioned that the assistant trainer position might open up, and we left it at that. He was impressed with . . . ," Ian hesitated, "my work with Gulfstream Waves."

"Gulfstream was a good horse," Samantha said softly. *I'm not mad at him anymore*, she realized. *What he did was just an accident, like Dad said.*

"But the best thing about the Townsends' offer is that we'll have our own cottage," Ian said. "I'll still be gone with the horses part of the year, but I don't think you'd have to travel with me and miss school."

"Maybe I could stay with Ashleigh," Samantha breathed. "Oh, I can't wait to get there!"

Ian looked directly at her. "Are you sure you're ready to leave Florida?"

Samantha thought about the blessing and love she had felt at her mother's grave. *Mom will always be with me, no matter where I go,* she thought. "Yes," she said firmly. "I think Mom would want you to take the job at Townsend Acres."

"I think so, too." Ian squeezed her shoulders. "It's settled, then. The position will open up in April. In the meantime we could go back to Aqueduct. You liked it there, didn't you?"

Samantha nodded. Beaming, she threw her arms around her father's neck. *I liked it there, and I liked riding there,* she thought. *I can't tell Dad that yet. But someday I'll make him understand—I know I can.*

13

SEVERAL MONTHS LATER, IN MID-APRIL, SAMANTHA STOOD just outside the mares' barn at Townsend Acres, trying not to jump up and down with excitement. "That's Ashleigh Griffen!" she whispered to herself. Ashleigh was across the stable yard near the training barn, talking to a big group of people who worked at Townsend Acres.

I can't believe how great it is here, Samantha thought. She gazed out at the luxurious farm, with its two huge, red barns for stabling the racing stock, manicured mile-long training oval, and acres and acres of rolling, white-fenced land. Overlooking it all was the Townsends' mansion on top of a rise.

Samantha shook her head. *That tack room at Finger Lakes seems like a bad dream.* She smiled, thinking of the snug, pretty cottage she and her father had moved into last night, right near the barns. And best of all, they were going to stay there for good.

Samantha squinted at Ashleigh's group. She recognized most of them from watching horse races on TV. The old man with the floppy hat was Charlie Burke, the trainer of Ashleigh' Wonder. The young, slender woman with the blond French braid was Jilly Gordon, who had ridden Wonder to victory in the Kentucky Derby. Jilly was one of the top jockeys in the country. The handsome young blond man was Ashleigh's boyfriend, Mike Reese, who trained at Whitebrook Farm.

They were all looking back at her! Samantha flushed. "Go over and introduce yourself," she said to herself. "No, I'd never dare!" Samantha turned quickly on her heel and darted into the mares' barn. She'd heard this morning that big news awaited in Wonder's stall.

Samantha walked slowly down the broad, immaculate barn aisle, reading the carved wood name tags attached to the front of the stalls. Most of the horses were out in the paddocks, enjoying the balmy spring day. "Mischief Maiden, Kelsey, Giselle," Samantha read aloud. "Ashleigh's Wonder . . ."

Hardly daring to, Samantha peeked inside Wonder's stall.

The Kentucky Derby–winning mare stood in the middle of the stall, holding her head low. Wonder's copper-colored coat gleamed softly, and she looked tired but content. She gazed at Samantha with her large, intelligent eyes.

"Hi, girl," Samantha breathed. *Wow—I'm really here,* she thought. *This isn't another dream.*

Lying on the straw close to Wonder was a compact bundle of copper-colored fur and long, stiltlike legs. Samantha had heard that the new foal's name was Wonder's Pride. "Wonder sure can be proud of you," she murmured. "You're absolutely perfect."

The foal stirred and opened his eyes. "Imagine trying to make you even prettier," Samantha said quietly.

"Hello," said a voice behind Samantha.

That's Ashleigh! Samantha jumped guiltily and gulped. She knew she had no right to be here. What if Ashleigh thought she'd disturbed Wonder and her foal? "I just wanted to see them," she said defensively. "Everyone was talking about them in the training barn."

Ashleigh smiled reassuringly. Samantha noticed how pretty Ashleigh was, with her hazel eyes and thick dark hair. *She's not much older than I am!* Samantha thought. She knew Ashleigh was only about seventeen.

"It's okay," Ashleigh said. "Wonder doesn't mind having admirers. Do you, girl?"

Wonder whickered in greeting, then stepped across the stall to nudge Ashleigh with her velvet nose. Wonder's Pride quickly wobbled after her.

Samantha stretched out a hand to the foal, then hesitantly drew it back.

"I'm Ashleigh Griffen." Ashleigh put out her own hand to Samantha. "You must be the new trainer's daughter."

Samantha shook Ashleigh's hand and nodded. "I'm Samantha McLean—but people usually call me Sammy. You sure it's okay I'm here?" she asked. Samantha knew how excited her dad was about this job. She couldn't get important people like Ashleigh mad at her.

"It's okay with me, and since I own half of Wonder and her foal, that's good enough," Ashleigh replied. "And you know, you can come here anytime you want. I know how hard it is to move to a new place. I had a hard time when my family first came here, but I think you'll grow to like it."

"I like it already," Samantha said softly, "though it's kind of hard not knowing anybody." She smiled uncertainly at Ashleigh.

Ashleigh smiled back. "Everyone who works here is pretty friendly. Where did you live before?" she asked.

Samantha shrugged. *It would take a really long time to tell Ashleigh that!* she thought. "All over the place. We moved around a lot, on or near different tracks— wherever my father could find a job."

"That must have been rough."

"It was," Samantha agreed. *But it's over now.* Relief

flooded Samantha so strongly, she had to grip the edge of the stall door to steady herself. "I think it's going to be better here," she said. "A farm is more like a home than a racetrack is."

Wonder's Pride had nestled in the straw to rest. But his bright dark eyes were fixed on Samantha.

Samantha looked back at the little colt. She could almost see him in a year, in two years . . . and as a great racehorse, thundering down the track at Churchill Downs and other famous tracks. She'd be part of it all.

I think this is going to be a great home. Samantha felt a broad smile stealing across her face. *What do you think, Mom?*

Epilogue

"SAMANTHA! THERE YOU ARE." TOR OPENED SHINING'S stall door and stepped inside. He sounded very relieved. "I looked everywhere for you."

Samantha gazed up into his face, startled. Shining was nudging her shoulder. For a moment Samantha hardly knew where she was. Then she remembered Cindy's terrible accident and shuddered. "Cindy?" Samantha asked, dread in her voice.

Tor sat down beside her and squeezed her hand. "Cindy's going to be okay. She ruptured her spleen and broke her arm—she's in serious condition at the hospital—but she's going to be just fine. Honor's shaken up, but she's all right, too."

"Oh, thank God." Samantha buried her face in Tor's shoulder, overcome with relief. "I was so afraid."

Tor stroked her hair. "It was a shock for you," he said. "I know how much you care about Cindy."

"Of course I do—she's my sister," Samantha said, her voice quavering. "I shouldn't have run away. But when Cindy fell . . . I just couldn't stand it. It reminded me so much of what happened to my mother. I was so sad and alone for so long after she died. . . ."

"Samantha, I'll always be here for you." Tor's voice was deep and reassuring.

He will, Samantha told herself. *He's here now. And Cindy's okay.* Samantha held tight to Tor's hand, letting the truth sink in. She drew a shaky breath. "How did you know I'd be in Shining's stall?"

"Your dad told me."

Of course. Samantha remembered the horrible morning so long ago when she had run to Miracle Worker's stall after her mother died and her world was shattered. "It's so hard to trust happiness," she said. "People you love can be taken from you so quickly. . . ."

"Can they really?" Tor asked gently. "Your dad's always saying how much you're like your mom."

Samantha closed her eyes, remembering her last trail ride with her mom so many years before. *Mom's there every time I enjoy a pretty day, the way we used to together, or when I ride a horse just the way she taught me,* Samantha thought. *And she'll always be there to love in my memories. We never said good-bye—but we didn't have to. It isn't good-bye.*

Samantha opened her eyes and smiled. "Someday I want you to say the same thing about me and my daughter," she said.

"Does this mean you still want to marry me?" Tor's expression was eager and hopeful.

"I still want to marry you." Samantha looked at him radiantly.

"Oh, Sammy," Tor whispered. "Kiss me."

Samantha threw her arms around Tor and tilted back her head to receive Tor's deep, passionate kiss. His mouth was sure on hers, and Samantha could feel the loving warmth of his embrace coursing through her body.

"Mmm," she murmured when they finally drew apart. "That was really, really nice."

"Now can we tell everyone our news?" Tor asked with a bright smile.

"I can't wait!" Samantha brushed away a last tear and took Tor's hand. She looked back at Shining. "You approve, don't you, girl?"

The beautiful mare snorted vigorously and bobbed her head, as if to say, "You bet I do."

JOANNA CAMPBELL was born and raised in Norwalk, Connecticut, and grew up loving horses. She eventually owned a horse of her own and took riding lessons for a number of years, specializing in jumping. She still rides when possible and has started her three-year-old granddaughter on lessons. In addition to publishing over twenty-five novels for young adults, she is the author of four adult novels. She has also sung and played piano professionally and owned an antique business. She now lives on the coast of Maine in Camden with her husband, Ian Bruce. She has two childern, Kimberly and Kenneth, and three grandchildren.

KAREN BENTLEY rode in English equitation and jumping classes as a child and in Western equitation and barrel-racing classes as a teenager. She has bred and raised Quarter Horses and, during a sojourn on the East Coast, owned a half-Thoroughbred jumper. She now owns a red roan registered Quarter Horse with some reining moves and lives in New Mexico. She has published thirteen novels for young adults.